Dean Judd's BOGGY BARRY.

A trilogy in one part.

Content Warning:

This book contains the subjects of depression and suicide.

Some of the ideas covered within the contents of this fiction novel cover topics of a sensitive nature. Reader discretion is advised to those sensitive to or may be affected by the subject of depression and suicide. The author will not be held responsible for any misconception over the subjects covered within this novel.

SPECIAL THANKS TO

Jake Smithies
for his constant support and help throughout
the progression of making this story into a book
for the past 3 years.
Also for his amazing concept of
Boggy Barry on the cover.

Heather Judd
For going through my world, tweaking what isn't
up to book publishing and writing standards and coming
out unscathed.
Also for being a fantastic wife who puts up
with my crazy shenanigans.

Baby Judd
Though you are not yet born and still
make Heather get me up at 5:30am to make her
bagels and cheese toasties, I thank you
for making me push myself in the right direction
of my career path as an artist.
You're a constant motivation for me and hope that one day
I can buy you a car.

Boggy Barry background.

My first university project was a "Frankenstein Project" where I had to find two pieces of artwork that inspired me and meld them together to make my own piece.
I was happy sticking to my digital art until my tutor had said this to me.

"Try something new, leave your comfort zone."
-Julie F. Westerman.

Boggy Barry was inspired by combining an unknown artist in London whose artwork was giant fabric sculptures oozing out expanding foam and Francis Bacon's "Three Studies for Figures at the Base of a Crucifixion, 1944".

Boggy Barry started off as a sculpture made from sponges, then covered in modroc and painted red for a fleshy exterior with yellow spikes sticking out of him. Trying something new also made me add nipples to Barry, something I never add to my work and is the only piece that includes nipples. Weirdly enough.

I then decided to compose a narrative for this creature I had created and the narrative is
"The Depressing Tale of Boggy Barry: The Over-Positive Abomination"
The story which you are about to read along with its sequels made years after.

The project was featured at the universities
"So Far So Good" exhibition, 08/12/14 – 14/12/14.
Hosted by Julie Westerman.

DEAN JUDD'S
Boggy Barry

The Depressing Tale of Boggy Barry:
The Over-Positive Abomination.

Part I

Sillitown is a nameless place. It hasn't bred any amazing actors or artists. It hasn't got any outstanding sights or any architectural breakthroughs. It won AppleCarrot Crumble of the year, sure – but only because they were the only contender and it was their own competition. However, they proudly state this on their welcome sign.

"WELCOME TO SILLITOWN.
Winners of AppleCarrot Crumble Contest of 1670"

Their government aren't much better; putting most of the funds towards military equipment and upgrading their base of operations with luxurious rest rooms, gaming rooms and spa treatments. Knowing fine well that no one will attack the small town of Sillitown. The civilians just work hard and have a peaceful life, completely unaware of their governments greed.

…Once upon a time, there lived an amazing scientist called Dr. Gigglesworth who just arrived out of nowhere.

Dr. Gigglesworth was a genius, well respected by everyone for his brilliant successes, particularly in creating a successful antidote for anxiety. He was a part-time clown, donating all his earnings to charity and lived on nothing but AppleCarrot crumble (without custard!) and loose green tea, which he would often share with the homeless and hungry.
However, Dr. Gigglesworth was an old man and he worried that the people he cared for would slip back into sadness when he passes. Would the hungry go without food? His donations would only go so far – would there be no money

for the charities? His lab notes- would people use them for evil and not for the good of man-kind? These questions deeply frightened Dr. Gigglesworth but then he came up with a remarkable idea!

If he created an everlasting clone of himself, which could work for the rest of eternity, he could pass peacefully knowing someone was doing what he did best; discovering new cures, donating to charity and feeding the hungry.

Immediately, Dr. Gigglesworth set about the task. He attempted various cloning experiments through his dusty incomplete old notes but every single one of them failed. He wasn't getting anywhere near his desired clone, and even though he was getting weaker every day, he held on to create his perfect heir. He started wondering whether there was a better way to pass on his legacy. Maybe instead, he wondered, could he make a creature? One he could teach to be good, one he could fill with love and positive emotions, he could make its appearance bright, colourful and soft for the children to play with. Dr. Gigglesworth was very excited about this, and he got to work right away!

A few days passed, Dr. Gigglesworth worked long and hard on his creation. At last, he envisioned a four-legged creature with a spongy, cuddly tail which he deemed 'Blissful Barry'. He made it so Barry could stand on his hind legs and use his front legs as arms to give the best hugs ever. His mouth was wide so he could give the biggest smile. Barry's skin was soft like pillows so he was super huggable. His voice was high and happy so he could sing lullabies to the children. Barry was also incredibly smart so he could come up with new cures for diseases and disorders and amazingly strong so he could help build town structures and houses.

Dr. Gigglesworth knew that a creature with this much positivity could become unruly, so Dr. Gigglesworth put golden needles of all sizes in Barry's insides that would ooze out negative feelings to help keep him calm and collected. This substance was known as "Liquid Negativity". Dr. Gigglesworth grew Barry in a large containment chamber that had the unborn creature hooked up to all sorts of machines, filling him with happiness and positive thoughts.

As Dr. Gigglesworth gazed at his creation, he began crying tears of joy, as he realized that humanity would be forever thankful to him for the birth of Blissful Barry, the Happy-Go-Lucky Masterpiece.

As he was crying, Dr. Gigglesworth didn't notice that Barry woke up – much earlier than anticipated – and began getting excited at the sight of his creator. He struggled to get free of the chamber to give Dr. Gigglesworth a huge "Hello Daddy!" hug, but the machines and wires held him fast. Dr. Gigglesworth panicked and tried to stop the machine, however, the machine had started to malfunction due to Barry's incredible strength. In the struggle, one of the machines claw arms went inside Barry's wide smiling mouth, pulling him inside out! The chamber filled with the blood of the creature and a terrible scream could be heard from inside. The scream pierced Dr. Gigglesworth's heart and he hung his head in sadness. He left the chamber room, believing his blissful Barry to be dead.

Moments later, footsteps could be heard from inside the chamber room. Dr. Gigglesworth scurried back, hope filling his heart, but he was greeted only by the sound of a creepy and eerie giggling. Wondering where the sound was coming from, Dr. Gigglesworth crept further into the room. The chamber was smashed open, and in the smoke, a silhouette of his beloved creature stood. Dr.

Gigglesworth was overjoyed – his creation had survived!

But then Barry stepped out from behind the smoke.

His appearance had shifted into something from a nightmare. The creature that stood before Dr. Gigglesworth was mostly red flesh. He had golden spikes piercing out of his body, oozing out black puddles of liquid negativity.

Dr. Gigglesworth's expression suddenly changed from one of joy to one of dread. In front of him stood not his creation, but a grotesque monster!

In attempt to escape, the old scientist ran to the door as fast as his weak muscles would allow. Barry saw the panicked expression on his creator's face and wanted nothing more than to cuddle him and make him feel better. With this intention, Barry stampeded toward Dr. Gigglesworth, screaming in a deep, spine-shivering voice of what could be deciphered as excitement. When he reached Dr. Gigglesworth, Barry stood up on his back legs and wrapped his front ones around Dr. Gigglesworth, and with his immense strength, crushed the bones in Dr. Gigglesworth's body, causing his entire skeletal system to collapse – killing him slowly and painfully.

Barry, being intoxicated with positive energy, had no idea he had ended the life of his creator. He only thought he was filling Dr. Gigglesworth with happiness, making him feel safe.

The needles sticking out of Barry started to ooze their negative liquids once more. This should have calmed Barry down, but due to the needles pointing out of him, little of the liquids made it into his system, and he maintained his overly positive attitude.

Barry left Dr. Gigglesworth's research facility singing a happy tune, promising the corpse of the scientist that he would return home in time for tea.

Barry headed into the town, skipping amongst the screaming pedestrians, who fled in fear. They knew nothing of Barry's good intentions, seeing him only as a terrifying monster that had somehow appeared in their lives. The people of the town thought that Barry wanted to terrorise and frighten them, when all he really wanted was to hug, play and sing with everyone.

People threw bottles at Barry, as well as verbal abuse, and he was even attacked by the police guards of the town. However, Barry was so overdosed on positive energy that he did not view these as attacks. In fact, he thought it was all one big game. So, Barry started doing what he was originally created to do – hug and make people feel happy. He whistled a happy tune as he hugged citizens of Sillitown, crushing their bones in the process.

The negativity in the needles still sticking out of Barry continued to ooze out at alarming rates, splashing all over the townspeople, spreading depression and sadness. Due to this, many of them did not care that there was a monster on a killing spree and even if any of them survived Barry's cuddles of death, they would end their own life after being exposed to even a little dash of the liquid negativity.

Dr. Gigglesworth made it so Barry could not be killed. So now this poor creature spends his days travelling from town to town, killing innocent people, spreading chaos and mass panic whilst under the illusion that he is really spreading joy and happiness.

If someone spent time examining Barry's behaviour and studied it, maybe they could find a way to calm him down- make him the creature he was supposed to be. However, one look at his fleshy, distorted appearance and everyone assumes he's just an ugly monster who wants nothing more than to kill.

Maybe if people could stop judging him by his appearance and took the time to know him, they could find out why he is acting this way. Maybe they could help him.

What must it be like ending the lives of many, destroying towns and civilizations but feeling as though you are doing the right thing? Killing people when you think you are making them happy? Being hated when you think you are being loved?

Barry continues his carnage, believing he is being kind, blinded by his own positivity.

This has been the Depressing tale of Boggy Barry: The Over-Positive Abomination. A misunderstood monster who just wants to spread happiness.

DEAN JUDD'S
Boggy Barry

The Heart-Warming Story
of Boggy Barry:
The Misunderstood Accident.

Part II

Three years had passed since the rampage of Boggy Barry, the over-positive abomination.

Following those catastrophic events, the government of Sillitown had captured Boggy Barry in secret and faked his death. Survivors of the attack were relieved and carried on with their lives. They began rebuilding the town and mourning over the death of the hundreds who were killed during Boggy Barry's rampage.

With Boggy Barry held in captivity at the government base, the members of the government saw an opportunity to expand their territory and become a stronger country. They went to war with neighbouring countries that they once were friends with, they sent Boggy Barry onto the battlefield. Barry's immense strength and needle-sharp skin killed any in his path and he was almost entirely bulletproof. He would stampede towards the terrified soldiers and would cuddle them to death, spewing his liquid negativity all around the battlefield, which made the soldiers feel weak with despair and depression, leading them to take their own lives.

After each battle the government would recapture him for the next fight. The citizens of Sillitown were completely unaware that their "*caring*" government would misuse the loving nature of this distorted monster to kill and expand their territory. They believed that the neighbouring countries were declaring war on them, and they applauded every new victory. "Our soldiers are the best!" They would cheer, completely unaware of the dark and selfish secret ; Held by the government.

However, someone had noticed something strange going on.

"The Disbelievers" were an underground group of rebels who thought it fishy that the country just happened to win every battle and without many casualties on their side. They thought it to be strange that all the neighbouring countries would declare war after years upon years of peace. There was something strange going on for sure, with the country and those who claimed to run it.

The Disbelievers consisted of five members, each with unique skills and specialities. First, there is Nikita Blue, a crafts girl with beautiful sapphire blue hair, eyes and lips to match. She can build anything out of everything; bombs, machines, computers, weapons - you name it! She wears gorgeous black dresses and sports a big gothic handbag full of who-knows-what. Nikita has a very caring nature and has a motherly aura about her despite baring no children. She always puts those she loves first and will stop at nothing to ensure their safety. The group jokingly used to call her "The Blue Mother" which she quickly put an end to as soon as it started, despite being the ripe age of 25, she couldn't stand the thought of her being a mother that young.

Then there's Layton Sherman Shake (or "Shake" for short) who is the medic, scientist and second in command. He can create any potion and heal any poison. He dresses rather formally: top hat and briefcase, both containing herbal remedies and valuable buffs. He is certainly a valued member, as the team healer. Shakes dress sense and overall appearance was something to be admired. He could wear muddied up carpets from an abandoned carpet shop, littered with insects and vermin and still pull it off. Shake is also Nikita's fiancée, not only do they act like they've been married for 50 years, but they squabble like siblings- a very bizarre but wonderful relationship. He once created a blue concoction that once drunk, causes the host to temporarily suffer a hang-over-like migraine for 50 minutes; he named it "The Blue Shake" in dedication to his blue haired fiancée.

There's Shivaria Ivy Cherry (Shivy for short), who is the hacker of the group. She can hack into any computer system, completely undetected - her friends call her The Cherry-Spyware. She's a very oriental character, wearing beautiful kimonos with long golden hair all the way down to her waist. Her eye-liner is always on point and her lips, redder than a ruby! Shivy and Nikita are like sisters, always laughing and joking about celebrities, clothes and make-up. She was born an only child in a rich family. Though her parents treated her like a princess, she certainly did not act like one. Though she doesn't act like a princess, she doesn't necessarily act like a "tomboy" either, coming over quite chilled, rebellious but full of manners

Roland Rocco Rix (or "Rix" for short) is the scout and spy of the group. He has contacts and connections in very high places and has easy access to inside information from a variety of reliable sources. He has long black and silver hair, most of it under an oil-stained burgundy beanie and overalls that just won't quit- he certainly stood out in the group. Rix is a very chilled and loyal character. He may have connections in various places but he would never give outside information on his group of rebels; he chooses his friends wisely and his connections even more so. Need a new phone? Ask Rix. Need to know the secrets in your sister's diary? Ask Rix. Need a lawyer for your upcoming case? You got it, ask Rix. Need to know how to get rid of make-up stains on the sofa? Probably best to ask Shivy…

Finally, there was the brains of the group: Larry Little - the leader and founder of The Disbelievers. A brave man who cared for everything except himself.

There was no man alive as selfless as he. He was highly respected among his peers, a natural born leader and he looked after his team. He sports a beautiful ginger mane powering out of the top of his head all around into a glorious beard, much like that of a proud lion. He has bulging muscles from his intense hobby of rock climbing and commonly wears vests and jeans; he wore basic clothing but had a unique way of thinking. Larry was always suspicious of the government ever since the Porkberry raid of '82, but what topped him off was a surviving solider from one of the wars. Rix had contact with the guy and after some intense interviewing, Larry (who had previously been a police interrogator, alongside Rix & Shake) believed every word this "mad man" had stated. "A happy-go-lucky monster on the field of battle?" he thought. "The death of our beloved Dr. Franklin Gigglesworth, then this? Could there be a connection?"

The Disbelievers had been watching the government closely for some time now, trying to work out what it was they were up to. After weeks of surveillance, they believed they were hiding a secret weapon at their headquarters. They had to stop them before more blood could be shed.

Larry Little declared, in order to find out, they must attack the base and storm the headquarters of the government head-on. The team was shaken up to even consider storming an impenetrable fortress like the headquarters of the government, but they knew Larry Little was right.

Nikita made a few "laughing gas bombs" and "smoke bombs". Shake prepared all his finest aiding kits and acids. Rix got the uniforms and maps from his good friend, Miss. Vanessa Lamb, from the inside and Shivy got all the passwords, usernames and even gained access to the security cameras on her beautiful pink and flowery tablet. With their fake IDs, they waited until the morning, dressed into their uniforms and they were ready.

Rix took the team to a secret back entrance, which he had located on the map and Shivy typed in the password to gain access. The door unlocked and they stepped inside. "So far so good", they thought.

They sneaked through stark white corridors and, though they were being cautious, it wasn't long before they were spotted by a patrolling blonde guard. Barely acting natural, they managed to walk away and avoided conflict and suspicion.

They passed a bright red door that said: "AUTHORISED PERSONNEL ONLY". From behind the door, Larry could hear faint screaming and moaning, mixed with an eerily happy whistling and humming - it was horrible listening to the mixture of emotions, but they needed to know what was behind the door. *"The happy-go-lucky monster?"* Larry thought.

Larry instructed Shivy to get them through- she used all her viruses and passwords but nothing worked. Shake tried some of his acid to burn through the door but it didn't work. Just then, a troop of guards came around the corner and they were spotted trying to get through the door!

One of the guards yelled, "Intruders!" and they began to open fire. Nikita launched one of her "laughing gas bombs" as the team dived behind a nearby metal crate, leaving the guards rolling around laughing uncontrollably!

Larry covered his face with the sleeve of his uniform to avoid being affected by the laughing gas, then ran over to one of the guards and pinched his security card. He swiped it through the access pad to the left of the door. It flashed red–denied.

The team realized that what was behind this door obviously could not be accessed by ordinary guards. Their curiosity amplified Shivy opened-up her tablet, looked at all the security cameras and found an empty control room that looked easier to access.

Larry ordered the team to go to the control room to open the door. They made their way there with their fantastic casual act and they were, thankfully, undetected. Shivy attempted to open the door with an override code, but it set off an alarm! Out of the many corridors, guards burst out with guns - Nikita threw one of her "smoke bombs" toward them, followed by a timed bomb of "laughing gas". The guards opened fire a few rounds and they managed to hit Larry in his right leg!

The team managed to escape in the smoke and in a matter of seconds, the "laughing gas bomb" went off, leaving all the guards powerless, holding their sides as they cried with laughter.
As they ran down the hall, Rix was carrying Larry as he couldn't walk.
"You okay there, dude?"
"I'm fine! We must find cover! Somewhere where the guards won't think to look!" stated Larry.
They ducked into the Ladies bathroom to recover.

As they were resting in the showers, Shake was treating Larry's wounds but it didn't look good. Oozing from his wounds were trials of gloopy, black liquid; a liquid Shake had never seen in all his years of science. "What's this then? Most unusual!" Shake exclaimed with upmost curiosity.

Suddenly, they heard footsteps coming into the bathroom – they readied themselves for an attack. A woman with long curly auburn hair wearing a lab coat walked in to the room - it was Vanessa Lamb! Rix instantly gestured for her to come over, and begged for her help. Vanessa Lamb had quite a high rank in the government and controlled a lot of the building. Surely she was a valuable contact to have as she also admired the work of Dr. Gigglesworth- such fantastic taste in heroes. Rix asked Vanessa if she could tell him anything about the big red door. She seemed to consider her words carefully. After a moment of silence, she said, "No one here knows what's behind that door and no one questions it. Only Dr. Crymore and his elite select guards knows." Lamb then noticed Larry bleeding on the floor, and the black liquid still dripping from his wounds - she gasped and jumped back in fear.

"The black liquid!" She cried, "Its Liquid Negativity! Don't touch it with your skin!"

The whole team looked confused. Lamb explained whilst breathing heavily that Liquid Negativity was a new form of weaponry that the government had been working on. Liquid Negativity is inserted into small bullets which, upon contact, spreads depression and suicidal tendencies throughout its host. "It takes a little while for it to actually kick in but if you survive the shots, you'll want to end your own life." She said, her voice full of sorrow.

The whole team gasped in shock and fear of this new information.

Rix and Shake helped Larry up and Rix cried, "Larry would never do that, he just wouldn't!"

Vanessa Lamb apologized and explained that it's what they have been working on. She said that she didn't agree with it, and had been trying to find a way to stop it herself, but she didn't have the authority. She asked if there was any way she could help - Rix instantly asked her to turn off the alarm and disable any alarms that might follow. She agreed and headed straight to the control room. Moments later, the alarm stopped.

Larry stood up and said in a cheery tone; "If it is true that in a matter of minutes I become incredibly depressed to the point where I am suicidal, we better cheer me up by getting to the bottom of this!" The team cheered at Larry's positivity. Shake bandaged up his leg and the team left the blood stained Ladies bathroom.

Getting back to work on the matter at hand, Shivy checked her tablet and found that there was a room called "Dr. Crymore's room."

The team headed into the elevator and rode up to the top floor - Floor 22. As they rode up, the elevator made many stops on the way, employees from other facilities and faculties shared the journey with them completely unaware of them being intruders. The employees were talking about work, home life and the ludicrous display on the match last night – some of the conversations were confidential and juicy.

One employee noticed the two stars and the words "Weapons Development unit" on our heroes name badges that Vanessa had supplied. The employee, who had five stars on his badge, wondered how five new members joined his facility of "Weapons Development" without him knowing. After a carefully worded statement from Rix saying how they were moved from another facility, the employee was more than happy to fill the Disbelievers on the progress they had made.

"Yeah well, 'our Kev, who oversaw the bullets, committed suicide due to getting a splash of that liquid negativity on 'imself, poor sod. Wearing gloves is strictly necessary in this line of work, but did ol' Kev listen? Nah, he were too busy eyein' up ol' Vanessa Lamb eating 'er Porkberry Pie 'nd mash, the pervy dingo – serves 'im right if I'm honest with yah, which I is!"

This man introduced himself as Calvin Husk, manager of the Weapons Development and in charge of Health and Safety, ironically, working closely alongside Vanessa Lamb.
He had short bleach blonde hair that curled at the fringe, he had an expensive diamond ear stud in his right ear lobe and a cocky smirk that seemed to say "I own this place."

"Aye, wait 'til ya meet Vanessa, she ain't 'alf a pretty 'un! I have dibs on 'er I tells yeh. I'm lookin' at you beanie boy, better watch yerself! Ahaha!" whilst pointing at Rix and his oil-stained beanie- despite being undercover, Rix refused to remove his hat.
Calvin was clearly a horrible man who had no regards for anyone but himself. Rix (who spent 3 years doing an acting degree before his enrolment in the forces). Decided to lower himself to this tool's level for the sake of the undercover
"Ah dude, I can't wait to start! I bet there's a lot of hot totty in this place, me best mate David Gulf in Military Operations says that there's a lot of girls in his

department and they're all right dirty! I'll 'elp you get with Vanessa, I'm one of the lands greatest wingmen you hear! Ahaha!" blurted Rix whilst winking and nudging occasionally.

Rix's performance was so outstanding that Calvin didn't even bat an eye at the rest of the group, Larry was showing signs of sadness in his face whilst the others were trying to console him.

"Mate! You get me with Vanessa and I'll make sure yah land a promotion in the next year or so, I can make dreams like that come true ya'hear! Me and Crymore were talkin' the other day about the progression with the creature we have contai- oh, here's my stop! See yah later alligator ya'hear!"

After Calvin left the lift, Rix let out an exhausted sigh. "What a tool," he expressed.

The elevator door opened and the team stepped out. Dr. Crymore's room was the only door in sight, right in front of them. Shivy checked that there were no security cameras in this room; seconds after revealing this Rix booted down the door with great force, and almost instantly, Nikita threw her final smoke bomb into the room. They dived in and listened for any coughing- there was none. Shake ran into the room and opened a window to disperse some of the smoke. The room was well kept, neat, tidy and empty. The team began rooting through drawers and files until they came across a red button hidden under Dr. Crymore's desk.

Larry pressed the big red button and through Shivy's tablet, they saw that they had unlocked the red door. Shake packed a bunch of the files labelled "CONFIENTIAL" in his suitcase and the team then headed back into the elevator.

"This is going well!" Shivy announced, her face beaming with positivity. Larry let out an exhausted chuckle, "We're doing well, everyone."

Suddenly, the elevator door opened on Floor 20 and in came the tool himself, Calvin.

"Bro! What you still doin' in this elevator man! You livin' in 'ere with these bozos? You lost or somethin'?"

Rix sighed and the act was back on. "Nah man, no way dude! Chill, just had to go to Crymore's office to do all that enrolment crap and he ain't in, what a bummer! So we're gonna kill some time and tour the place, you feelin' me?"

"Ah man, Crymores such a tool yah 'ear me? He fired me main bro Leonard McGrovell because he leaked information to outsiders about the creature we have contained in the Red Room producin' all that sweet sweet liquid negativity, he wasn't happy, man – haven't seen 'im since ya'hear!"

Wow. He really was a tool.

"Calvin bro, I hear yah! Me last boss fired my now ex-girlfriend…"
Rix proceeded to give Calvin a cheeky nudge and wink.
"…for providing free food to poor homeless women, I mean I don't blame dah boss – how's that makin' any dough!?"
"Dude that sucks that she wasted the company's time like that! Anyway, bro this is my stop, see you later for your introduction in weapons development! No promises I'll be sober for it, yah hear!"

"I hear yah bro, may join yah ahaha! Later!"

The door shuts on floor 10 and Rix lets out a heavy sigh. "If I ever see that man again, I may just smack him." he exclaimed.

Shivy checked the cameras once again and noticed that some giggling guards around the red door were helping the guards who were still having a laughing fit. They knew they were outnumbered so Shake handed Nicky some ingredients, they had just enough to create a small laughing gas bomb. Although with laughing being so contagious, this amount of laughing gas should be enough - the elevator door opened just in time for Nikita to finish the bomb, she threw it at the guards instantly. The bomb exploded, leaving all of the guards to fall about laughing.

The team ran past them, through the big red door and found themselves in a long corridor lit by red lights. Larry was quick to lock the door behind them, then suddenly an eerily happy whistling of something in pain echoed off the walls.

Halfway down the corridor, Larry started to cry. As tears began to well in his eyes he wailed, "I don't think we're going to make it! What if we fail and we all get captured and tortured! It'll be all my fault!"
Knowing this was Liquid Negativity starting to take effect, Nikita gave Larry a big hug and told him that everything was going to be alright. The group joined in comforting him. Larry shook off his sudden sadness and the team continued, pointing out how great they were doing so far and how this day has certainly been an adventure. Shake even took it upon himself to do an amazing impression of Calvin, oh how the team laughed!

"Hey, I'm Calvin and I just revealed classified information to a bunch of strangers in a lift, I'm a complete tool! Ya'hear me!?"

The end of the corridor loomed into sight, and opened out into a huge room, full of lab notes, computers and machinery. They were in awe of the sheer size of the space and the array of scientific equipment that adorned it.

Then, they saw him.

In the middle of this dark room, surrounded by computers, metal crates and desks - they saw Boggy Barry.

He was encased in a dangling electronically charged cage, being painfully zapped every few seconds. Each spark made him squeal in pain, closely followed by eerie giggles and a cheerful whistle. On the floor surrounding Boggy Barry was a deep hole, covered in pipes that lead to giant metal crates, capturing the pitch-black Liquid Negativity that squirted out of Barry's spikes as he got zapped.

The team were a little frightened of Barry, but they hated seeing him suffer. Shake instantly ran towards the lab notes. Amidst them, he found *the depressing tale of Boggy Barry*. He read it aloud to the team and they were all taken aback by the tale of this creature. Hearing about Dr. Gigglesworth's failed attempt to create a happy creature didn't sit well with Larry, who was now borderline suicidal. In a fit of rage and overwhelming sadness, Larry ran towards Boggy Barry's cage in attempt to shock himself to death. Just in time, Rix grabbed hold of him and pulled him away.

Without warning, the lights in the room came on and coming down an elevated platform, was none other than the black and red formally dressed young gentleman, himself, Dr. Crymore.

Dr. Crymore shouted, "Ahhh, the Disbelievers! I was wondering when I'd finally meet you! Been quite the little pests, haven't we?"

Larry pulled free of Rix's grasp and looked upon Dr. Crymore with tears in his eyes and shouted, "What is the meaning of this, Crymore?!"

Dr. Crymore chuckled and said, "What you see before you, is our secret weapon. Our success. Our reason for domination. What you see before you is Boggy Barry, my brother's masterpiece!"

The whole team gasped in shock. Shake shouted "You're... you're Dr. Gigglesworth's brother!? *THE* Dr. Gigglesworth!?"

Crymore began laughing and shouted back, "Yes, yes I am. My brother was a fool, an idiot - he put all his research in curing the brainless public, he fed the worthless hungry and he danced for the pathetic brain-dead children. He didn't think about using his brains for profit-for domination, like me!"

Doors from both sides of the room swung open and a team of over 100 guards came pouring out, pointing their guns at the team. Vanessa Lamb jumped out of an observation window onto the platform where Dr. Crymore was standing and attempted to place a highly explosive bomb onto him. Dr. Crymore knocked it out of her hands and pushed her off the platform with great ease and sass. She landed and banged her head on the railings.

Rix rushed over to help, dragging her away from Dr. Crymore, who was shaking his head as if in disgust.

"This thing is a creature of war!" Crymore screamed, pointing angrily at Boggy Barry. "A creature of chaos and destruction! Are you so cruel to release it upon the public so it can continue its horrific massacre!? Remember what happened three years ago!? What kind of people would do that to their country? Terrorists, that's who!" he added

Whilst Crymore was ranting and raving, the bomb he had knocked out of Vanessa Lamb's hands had rolled over towards where the team now stood. Larry saw an opportunity to end all of this. Dr. Crymore was a madman- there would be no reasoning with him.

Larry screamed and ran towards the bomb, shrieking "Save the research, save the truth, save Barry and get out of here!"

He attached the bomb to himself and ran towards Dr. Crymore and the guards. The guards shot at him, but Larry Little kept running, tears brushing off his face. Dr. Crymore realised what Larry was about to do and ducked behind one of the nearby metal crates in attempt to cover himself from the blast. He thought he was safe. Then Larry exploded.

The blast took out a whole section of the room revealing sunlight from the outdoors, and the ceiling began collapsing in on itself. Dr. Crymore scrambled and limped away from the falling debris, towards Boggy Barry's cage. He tried to run but as he did, a piece of rubble fell from the ceiling and landed onto one of the metal crates containing Liquid Negativity! The crate was knocked over and black liquid flooded all over Dr. Crymore. He screeched in agony as the liquid came into contact with his skin.

Debris kept falling and just before he was crushed by it, Crymore shouted "I shall return and when I do – the world will be mine!"

The guards and Crymore were lost in a haze of dust and mountains of rubble. What was left of the room was a complete mess. The team had survived by hiding under the desks - Shake had grabbed all the research notes, Nikita and Shivy looked after each other and Rix had saved Vanessa Lamb.
They looked over and saw Boggy Barry dancing around in his electric cage, looking happy and excited like there was nothing wrong with the world - the cage was still active, however, and was still zapping him, causing him great pain.

They had a moment of silence in dedication to Larry Little, their fallen hero. Wondering, did Larry Little blow himself up because he was suicidal? Or did he blow himself up to save everyone? The team, of course, believed the latter- he saved them. Shake turned away and began reading the research notes, Rix was taking care of Vanessa Lamb and Nicky and Shivy were disabling the electric cages shocking treatment so Barry wouldn't get hurt. They had no idea what to do with Boggy Barry; they couldn't just release him, as he'd kill everything in his path again. Then Shake had an idea. "Guys! These are the notes used to create Barry!" The team looked confused. "What if we create our own Boggy Barry?" Shake continued. "One that could help and understand the original Boggy Barry, calm him down and help him understand what is going on? We have the notes on how Gigglesworth did it!"

The team cheered with excitement! Rix instantly got in contact with one of his friends from the military – Daniel Chopper Comrade, a strapping young lad with a Mohawk and a blonde lightning bolt dyed on the side of his head. He wore military gear and mainly pink camouflage attire. In what felt like no time at all, a huge chopper flew over and picked the team up, carrying the cage holding Barry, with a cloth draped over it to prevent the public from seeing him.

The chopper arrived at the gaping hole at the side of the building. As they flew away back to their hideout, the doors to this dark, despicable room covered in liquid negativity and rubble opened and in came the employees who were in complete awe of the devastation. Calvin clenched his fist, looking at the distant silhouette of a chopper and picking up a discarded lab-coat the the name tag "Rix" on it, he whispered "I'm gonna get you Beanieboy lad, you 'ear me?"

Daniel Comrade returned the team to their headquarters but left quickly without a word, like he was in some sort of a rush. Shake and Rix began debating what creature to create. Meanwhile, Nikita and Shivy moved Barry to a special room with a pit, which was collecting all the Liquid Negativity, still spewing out of him - he was still caged but Shivy disabled the electric current so that he wasn't being harmed. Nikita and Shivy noticed that the Liquid Negativity was coming from Boggy Barry himself and realized that the government must have been extracting it from him to make the bullets that led Larry to his death. They relayed this information back to Shake, who noted that whatever creature they were to make, it must be able to withstand the effects of the Liquid Negativity.

Weeks went by, but the team had no idea how they were going to create this creature. They dabbled with making Barry a parental figure creature to teach

Barry disciple, but it may cause him to rebel against them. Maybe they could remove the golden spikes?

No, not only is it extremely dangerous to be around the Liquid Negativity spewing spikes but its the only substance that would calm Barry down.

The team were in dire need of a distraction, completely over thinking the situation was getting them nowhere until one day, Rix and Vanessa Lamb came over and they announced that they were expecting a baby!

The whole room cheered and they congratulated the couple with plenty of Dove Milk Wine and Loaf Lettuce Noodles.

"If its a boy, we're calling him Gigglesworth Jr after my hero, Dr. Gigglesworth!" Vanessa said.

"Annnnnddd if its a wee lassie, she'll be Diamond-Chariot Rix!" Rix announced proudly as the team gagged at Rix's child name. In secrecy, Vanessa begged and bargained the fetus to be a boy.

Shake giggled at the beautiful scene and the wonderful names then, like finding the missing piece to a big puzzle - Shake clicked. He had an idea.

He ran to the lab and started to get to work. The team followed and saw him frantically begin to work on an experiment. When they asked what he was doing he shouted, "I AM A GENIUS!"

The team were intrigued. They looked upon Shake's computer screen and saw his brilliant idea start to take effect. The creature he was creating was none other than a baby. They watched as the lab machines started building this little baby creature. They whizzed and whirred and pumped liquids into a chamber.

After a few days and a lot of clanging, banging, whirling and smashing, the chamber door opened and out waddled a little baby creature.

It was the most adorable little thing you have ever seen.

It had sponge-like yellow skin, rectangular limbs and a salmon pink quadrilateral shaped tail. His eyes were huge baby blue pools of fun, his mouth wide and cheerful and the neat little bundle of skin around his waist resembled that of a diaper.

The team were in awe of its endearing design and *"aww'ed"* in perfect sync, making the baby giggle and snort in a cute voice.

Shake began explaining what he had created:

"A baby is exactly what Barry needs." He said. "Whenever the baby starts crying, Barry will hug it, which would cause death for us, but I have made sure that the baby's skin is made of a sponge-like cushion and therefore he will not die. I have made it so that when the baby is hungry, he will want to drink Liquid Negativity and like a baby to the mother's teat, the baby will drink the Liquid Negativity out of Barry's spikes."

The team were flabbergasted.

"Whenever the baby is full, he will emit a gas, converting Liquid Negativity into Positive Gas!" Shake continued. "Those in the gas will feel so much better and depression will be a thing of the past."

"That's amazing, Shake!" Shivy said. "You have completed Dr. Gigglesworth's dream!"

Shake followed up with, "Having this baby will give Barry responsibility, thus calming him down. The only thing we need to hope for is that Barry falls in love with the baby..."

The team took the cute little baby into Barry's room, wearing protective suits so that the Liquid Negativity wouldn't touch them.

Barry laid eyes on the baby and almost instantly, he started wailing in happiness. He became ruthless, thrashing around the cage and dancing and cheering in excitement - Liquid Negativity was going everywhere! Shivy quickly opened the cage using her hacking skills and Barry ran straight towards the baby and gave him a big hug. The team were cheering! The plan had worked!

The baby jumped out of Barry's grasp and began rolling in the Liquid Negativity, giggling. Barry, in a playful manner, joined the baby in rolling and they both absorbed every last bit of the black liquid. Barry was finally able to calm down, then the baby emitted the gas and the whole room was filled with positivity. Everyone was so happy and cheerful. Nikita then turned to Shake and asked, "Does the baby have a name?"

The team looked at each other, looked towards the baby and in perfect, unexpected sync said, *"Little Larry"*.

After finally getting the general public's acceptance and a good couple of months passing, the whole world was at peace thanks to Little Larry and Barry. There were no more feuds with neighbouring towns and cities, only trust and tranquillity.

Barry and Larry would wander around the land spreading positivity, helping as many people as they could and in the first year of public debating, Rix and Lamb had their child. They called him Gigglesworth Jr and he became Barry and Larry's very best friend.

This whole catastrophic tale of a giant four-legged fleshy, spiked covered beast and its little baby may have brought a handful of visitors and tourists to the nameless town of Sillitown, however not enough for them to change the welcome sign to something like

"SILLITOWN. Home to Barry and Larry!"

No, they're still winners of the AppleCarrot Crumble contest.

So very silly.

DEAN JUDD'S
Boggy Barry

The Legend of Boggy Barry:
The Redeemed Masterpiece.

Part III

has been three whole three years since the redemption of Boggy Barry, "The Misunderstood Accident". Barry now frolics around the land with his cheery spongy son, Little Larry, who drinks Barry's liquid negativity from his golden sharp spikes to produce a gas of positivity through his spongy pink tail- doing the complete opposite to what Barry was like all those years ago.

The "Disbelievers" are now managing the land as the government, they are now known as "The Saviours" as they risked their very lives to show the land the truth as to what was going on with those who were in control.

"THE GOVERNMENT'S DARKEST SECRET LEAKED!" The newspapers titled, *"BARRY AND SON CURE DEPRESSION WITH NEW AND **FREE** POSITIVE GAS!"* they would add.

The Saviours are highly respected members of the community and consist of six members now, there is the computer hacker herself: Shivaria Ivy Cherry, the gadgeteer: Nikita Blue, the man who always knows a man: Roland Rocco Rix, the helicopter pilot: Daniel Chopper Comrade and finally the scientist, medic and new leader of the group: Layton Sherman Shake and his lovely assistant Vanessa Lamb who, is now a parent with Rix of their beautiful son, known as Gigglesworth Jr.

Daniel Comrade quickly became a member of the Saviours after helping them transport Barry from Dr. Crymores secret laboratory in great haste. He returned to their base weeks later, requesting to be a full-time member which they happily agreed upon.

Speaking of Dr. Crymore, they never found his body! Could it have been crushed by the rubble? Could it have been burnt into an unrecognisable pile of ash? Could he have somewhat escaped? The police investigated and only found an arm and a leg from different sides of the room due to the blast; maybe the rest of Dr. Crymore has been blown away? If he did escape he couldn't have gotten very far, surely?

Lamb and Rix's son, Gigglesworth Jr. is now two-years of age, always laughing, sharing and just generally a ball of sunshine- he's a smarty-pants too! Gigglesworth Jr. is always playing with Barry and Larry. Barry is extremely protective and will do all he can to lookout for both Gigglesworth Jr. and Larry. Gigglesworth Jr better stay clear of Barry's golden spikes though!

Within the three years of The Saviours being in power, wonderful and fantastic things have happened! The Scientists Shake and Vanessa Lamb managed to create the same system that Gigglesworth had constructed to create Barry. With this knowledge, Shake and Vanessa Lamb had created 8 unique creatures that resemble that of Barry, but each with their own unique function and abilities to benefit society!

These magnificent beings are known as "Colossi". The eight Colossi include:

The fiery tempered and vain, Amber. Amber resembles that of a blood orange lioness; she has a beautiful burning mane which can disperse heat, which is very useful when in freezing cold climates as she can adjust the temperature to the right point to warm people up. She can breathe fire (to an extent) which is of course used for defending the town or creating a source of fire when required. She has a roar that can be heard for miles; this thunderous roar may have a vast range of projection, however, is friendly towards the ears of nearby folks without the need of ear defenders. She can jump far and carry up to four people on her back, making her also useful for scouting tricky terrain.

We have the energetic and dozy Farad. Farad is a yellow, humanoid colossi with custard coloured elastic skin; his skin can be manipulated by stretching into the form of any output/input that needs plugged in. Farad can generate electricity by being very active and generally being in a good mood and, with no extra cost to his energy, he has a beautiful dimly-lit glow about him, making him easy to spot in the dark. Farad may have legs and feet, but on his feet, he has wheels that allow him to get around very fast and in doing so, makes him less active but puts him in a great mood almost instantly! His tongue is one of his best features. Not only is it a fantastic conductor but it has amazing wireless charging capabilities, allowing people's battery powered devices to charge whilst being around him.

We have the peaceful and calm Woodroe. Woodroe's skin resembles that of bark from trees; he has a huge tree on his back and a glorious vine moustache and bushy beard. Woodroe's feet plant seeds when he steps and his overall aura helps the plants grow; he can also emit beautiful ranges of scents which have been known to relax and calm people down. Woodroe not only provides Shake with herbs for his medical duties, he also grows vegetation so the land is a lot healthier due to free vegetables freshly grown by Woodroe himself. Woodroe also supports huge antlers from atop his crown, allowing him to fend off unwanted predators when prey animals dine on his vegetation. With this, prey animals have become more comfortable around humans, allowing wild deer sightings to increase and other shy critters much easier to get closer to and observe

We have the bubbly Bubbles. Bubbles looks like that of Amber and Woodroe but resembles the form of a Brachiosaurus; he has a long neck which he uses to accurately read temperatures and for looking out into the ocean for anyone who maybe struggling at sea. Bubbles' body can inflate like a life boat; he can swim and dive at rapid speeds making him a saviour to stranded citizens. His camel-humped back is distinguished as he travels the desert, along with Woodroe, to created oasis's for stranded travellers. His tail is like a water cannon, which also has a sprinkle mode for those hot summer days. Much like Amber, Bubbles too can adjust the temperature by dispersing cold air to cool a place down if it is too hot. Amber and Bubbles have their differences but they get along like an old married couple! Bubbles' voice sounds like trying to talk whilst gaggling water, except on a pro level.

We have the "Pink Twins", Lisa and Amy. Lisa and Amy pretty much come as a pair; they're twins in a sense and were created at the same time, unintentionally. Both are the same beautiful pink colour but their roles in the world are ever so slightly different. Lisa acts like a bus or a tram, transporting people and luggage around the town by running through her own designed routes; as she runs, her body stays very still making passengers not feel sick or affected by the high speeds. She also has a sensitive roof over her back which has tiny ear and microphone holes so that her passengers can ask her to stop at their desired location. As she announces when she is stopping she will even crack a joke or two! Her humour, however, is as dry as a desert that Bubbles and Woodroe had missed.

Amy, of course much like Lisa, is made for transportation however she takes to the skies. She flies through the air like a plane with her gorgeous pink feathered wings taking people abroad and delivering parcels to other nearby countries and distant lands. Amy is always in contact with Lisa through some kind of "Twin ESP" this makes allowing tracking each other very easy. They're a cheeky twosome but valued highly by society.

We have the bouncy and fun-loving Funple. Funple is the biggest Colossi out of the whole gang, in fact he's bigger than a house and is pretty much a giant, walking, living amusement park! His tongue has a huge ladder which leads up to his forehead which too has a ladder up his head. His back and tail is like a track for the small purple lumps which act as carts, like those of a roller-coaster. His arms can extend extremely wide, his wrists dislocated from his hands allowing them to rapidly spin around whilst people are sitting on the mounted chairs upon his fingers. His feet inflate like a bouncy castle, his arms and legs play bouncy music and colourful lights glow out of his shoulders, hands and knees. Health & Safety is Funple's number one priority so he makes sure everyone is having fun, safely. Funple also has two other special abilities: he can eat sound and transform anything loud, silent. He can also play any sound effect there is. Being this big, Funple rarely walks about and usually stays stationary however he doesn't mind the occasional walk. Funple was merely an experiment to see how big they could make a Colossi; they didn't really intend him to be this huge, however, he remains a Sillitown favourite.

Finally, we have the motherly Cecilia Ramaysa. Cecilia Ramaysa is a very, very important Colossi as she acts like a walking, talking, constantly recording super computer. She is transparent with a frosty touch of white; her skin his covered in small bendable screens which can display anything from an internet browser or playbacks from her own recording devices. Cecilia Ramaysa, for obvious reasons, has two extremely well trained and armed, trustworthy security guards who watch over her; because if the wrong hands gets hold of her, the land could be in great peril.

~ ~ ~

The neighbouring lands with whom country once quarrelled with have patched things up and became once again alliances thanks to The Saviours. Shake has promised that once they can be sure that the science can be respected, they will openly share information of the Colossi creation process, however for now, they will continue creating Colossi to benefit the world. Shake and Vanessa Lamb have more ideas regarding Colossi; they have Colossi plans to prevent world hunger, diminish pollution and even one that detects upcoming natural disasters! Everything in Sillitown was going very smoothly; positive gas was in the air, children were growing up with Funple, learning the importance of safe play and everyone was getting a decent education thanks to Cecilia Ramaysa- everything was great!

Until...

Amber, who was on the outskirts of Sillitown let out a huge roar, which was heard by The Saviours. The team rode their way, on the back of Amy, to investigate the scene, accompanied by Barry and Larry. What they saw shook them up.

There was bodies, loads of bodies. And worst of all, there was black liquid all over the field! Amber was shaken up and tried to tell The Saviours what she had witnessed, "They just started killing each other... and once they killed a few people, they killed themselves!" The team gasped as Shake looked at the liquid suspiciously. "We need to get the black liquid off the field, then we shall have a proper burial." announced Shake.

"Don't you mean get rid of the Liquid Negativity, Shake?" asked Nikita. Shake shook his head and said "Amy, go and bring Bubbles here please. We need him to get rid of this black substance." Amy nodded and responded with "Yes sir!" and she flew off back towards the town.

Shake sat down next to Amber whilst Nikita who is very close to Amber, stroked her fiery mane. Shake turned to Amber, "Did you see anything else?" Amber pondered for a few seconds before her mane lifted.
"I saw an unsymmetrical silhouette walk away from the scene!"
Nikita asked Shake what he thought is going on. Shake just sighed and took a step back staring at the massacred scene once again, too deep in thought to answer Nikita.

Nikita was very used to this behaviour- he's like this at breakfast. "Would you like Pancakes or Toast with your Rhubarb spread?" Shake would rise from his seat and pace up and down their dining room, stating "Let me consider both these options....". It's one of Nikita's pet peeves of Shake- so dramatic.

Bubbles arrived on the back of Amy; she dropped him off like a giant rain droplet as he *splooshed* onto the ground. Shake waved at Amy as she flew away. He then asked Bubbles if he could wipe away all the black substance and

Bubbles complied at once.

Bubbles is not really used to this kind of sight; however, he is used to cleaning up rather unusual stains. Bubbles is the kind of colossi that just wants to get work done and get it done right.

Bubbles raised his arm and tail revealing the sprinkler and cannon. He watered down the substance but it was tough to get rid of, so he switched from sprinkler to blaster which removed the substance much easier. Shake stopped Bubbles from spraying before approaching the final puddle of the liquid as he then brought out a test-tube. The team shouted and screamed for him to get away from it, but something didn't feel right to Shake. So he put on some gloves and scooped up the substance.

The team collected the identities of the victims and got in touch with their families. They had a moment of silence for the poor victims after burying the, now clean, bodies. The Saviours left the scene in distraught and went back home- everyone apart from Shake. Shake stayed up all night with Cecilia Ramaysa, conducting experiments with the "liquid" they had found at the scene. Then Shake had made a shocking discovery!

A meeting was held just for the Saviours in their main headquarters- everyone attended in the early morning with their own hot beverages: Shivy with her all natural, loose green tea, Rix with a hard black coffee with 3 sugars and half a sweetener, Daniel with a typical builders tea, Nikita with a glass of hot water and a slice of lemon in a wine glass and Vanessa Lamb with a glass of hot Dove Milk and a slice of Raspberry Pork for a late breakfast. Then enters the sleep-deprived Shake, clutching a black coffee and smoking barely extinguished cigarette.

"What's going on, love?" asked Nikita Blue.

"Are you okay Shake?" added Shivy as she inhaled the scent her of her sweet green tea. Shake stubbed out his cigarette, put his coffee down and lit a new cigarette.

"Is it about the massacre last night, dude?" asked Rix who is barely awake,

"Yeah, I couldn't sleep a wink last night - Gigglesworth Jr seemed distraught too...." added Vanessa Lamb. Shake turns his head and looks towards the door and sighs. In comes Cecilia Ramaysa, not looking at all chirpy, unlike her usual self.

"Thank you all for coming so early and at such short notice. Last night I had made a shocking discovery which will change the course of our current experiments." said Shake, gravely.

"Have you found the cure for Liquid Negativity, Shake!?" Vanessa Lamb asked enthusiastically, "Was it the tea-leaves and custard? I had a feeling it would be them!" she added whilst she took a heavy dose of her milk.

"Sadly not Vanessa Lamb, no. I'm afraid what I have discovered is bad news." said Shake.

"What is it?" questioned Nikita, expecting to be ignored again. At this point, Cecilia opened-up her wings, displaying two giant screens with two substances rotating and dripping.

"Well, during the clean-up of the substance, we found at the scene, I felt very uneasy and unsettled by the way the substances was reacting to the water, so I decided to scoop up some of the substance, as you well know. Last night I started to experiment out of curiosity. When Amber said she saw them all kill themselves, I thought like everyone else did - just a depressing side-effect of liquid negativity but sadly, this is not the case," explained Shake.

"Oh give it a rest, Shake! Stop story-telling and give us the facts!" interrupted

Daniel Comrade.

Shake slammed his hands down and stared Daniel down, "I was up all-night risking my life, toying with these liquids, how about you have the decency to let me finish, Comrade!"

Daniel slammed down into his chair with his arms folded like a child having a tantrum, "I'm sorry, please proceed." mumbled Daniel. "Now, I realized that this liquid isn't a full-on liquid, it's a tar-like substance. Liquid negativity is water-based, it flows with water when washed away, however the substance at the scene was in-fact different. I originally thought it was just hardened Liquid Negativity however, Amber stated it must have came from the unsymmetrical silhouette leaving the premises which wasn't too long ago before we turned up," continued Shake before taking a long harsh drag of his cigarette, "When Bubbles was washing away the substances, it was ripping and peeling off the ground and not flowing with the water- it had to be different I thought, hence why I scooped it up and after a long night of experimenting - its bad news." Shake added. The team clutched hold of their chairs, "This is an advanced form of Liquid Negativity."

The team gasped, not believing what they had just heard, "What!? How!?" questioned Vanessa Lamb, "Liquid Negativity leads people to depression and suicidal tendencies. This liquid leads people to feel an uncontrollable feeling of rage and blood-lust. After the rage and blood-lust, the victims conscious mind and negativity will kick in and instantaneously lead them to kill themselves however way they can." The team couldn't believe what they were hearing.

"Where did it come from?" asked Rix.

"What's it called?" muttered Daniel.

"Can you cure it?" enquired Shivy.

"I have no name for it yet and no, I'm afraid not. It looks like it'll be harder to cure than Liquid Negativity. I have however, found the key-chemical is in fact 'Kamikaze Khemical ', a chemical found on "Kamikaziants".

Kamikaziants are a breed of black ants that let out a black tar-like chemical that drives other ants to go on a vicious rampage. When they infiltrate an enemy nest, the Kamikaziant run in as far as they can, getting bitten left, right and centre until they die. Upon death, their remains let out a little the chemical which infects the soil. When a dozen or so ants walk over the tar, it doesn't take long for the ants to turn on each other and rip each other apart.
Kamikaze Khemical won't have this effect on humans or bigger animals, but can be quite poisonous in huge doses. Only mixed with Liquid Negativity, will the blood-lust effect take place with humans.

"It looks like this fluid is basically Liquid Negativity, just with that added chemical." said Shake.
 "Only us, Dr. Gigglesworth and Dr. Crymore knows how to make Liquid Negativity, right? Who else knows how to make it?" asked Shivy.
 "That's the question I've been asking myself all night..." replied Shake "Trying to find its composition is pretty difficult and highly dangerous" he added.
"But seriously, what are we going to call this fluid that releases our inner fury?" asked Daniel.
 "...Fury Fluid?" asked Rix, raising an eyebrow.
 "I like it" said both Daniel and Shake in perfect sync.

They shared a small giggle and then Shake said quite enthusiastically as he sparked up another cigarette "That's all the information I have for you all today, I'll continue researching and see if I can find anything else after the Fruit and

Veg Fair - Woodroes birthday.".

The Fruit and Veg Fair is a very special event in the small town of Sillitown, it's in a way like Christmas but instead of looking forward to the huge fattening meals and treats, it's all about the detox and experimenting with new fruits and vegetation. When Woodroe was born, he began growing his vegetation and fruits and happily gave them away. A whole day was spent with people making vegetable smoothies, fruity cocktails and extraordinary salads. Everyone was sharing recipes and generally got along with such unity. They then decided that it will not only keep getting bigger each year, but it was going to be a national holiday. Last year, for example, stalls were introduced and merchandise was created in dedication to the fair and the year after that, the whole town changed their lights to a green colour, the water features, the street lights – everything!
What will this year bring I wonder?

"I can't wait for the Fruit and Vegt Fair this year, it's going to be great!" said Shivy as she clapped her hands like an excited child.

"I've been craving a lot of healthy food recently, I'm going to gobble up the feast myself!" said Nikita Blue, sucking on her lemon. The team continued to giggle as they were discussing the Fruit and Veg Fair. The team left the meeting room; Shivy went to help Woodroe with the Fair, Shake went to get some rest, Lamb and Rix took Gigglesworth Jr. to play with Funple, Barry and Larry and everyone else went home.

The Fruit and Veg Fair was only two days away and there was a lot to prepare for. Lisa and Amy where transporting many various kinds of fruit and veg from all over the land, Bubbles was setting up the water features, Farad was preparing the electric signs and Amber was in charge of the warm air and atmosphere. The preparation was going very well until Woodroe and Shivy started to harvest the veg from the other side of the party field, completely out of sight of the others. As Shivy was plucking the AppleCarrots, there was a rustling from the bushes in the forest in front of the farm. Woodroe brushed it off as he thought it could have been an animal attracted to his green aura, however Shivy's tablet started rapidly beeping, alerting her there was *"Programmic life"* about - she looked around and couldn't see Cecilia Ramaysa anywhere so she clicked on the result, which had a name displayed.

A figure popped out of the bushes and all they saw was a steel head with a grinning design upon it. Woodroe wandered cautiously towards the figure showing off his huge antlers, however when he had gotten close he got blasted in the face with Fury Fluid! He swung side to side before slamming into the ground! Shivy screamed, keeping her eyes on at the bushes, when in her vision she saw a black ball of Fury Fluid fly towards her, but before it could hit Shivy, Barry jumped in between her and the ball! Being the strongest Colossi, he wasn't sent back by the force. Barry checked to see if Shivy was okay before running towards Woodroe and helped him up. Both Woodroe and Shivy were very shaken up by the whole ordeal. "Thank you, old friend...." said Woodroe in a soft, out of breath tone.

The Saviours came running towards them to see if they were okay. They noticed Woodroe was covered in Fury Fluid so Bubbles gave him a wash. Shivy explained to the team what she had saw, "I detected programmic life in the area, upon reading the devices name, I became paralysed!" Shivy said.

"What did the name say, Shiv?" asked Nikita Blue, Shivy took a deep breath as silence filled the air.

"CRYBORG."

Everyone was blown away. Rix was the first to point out, "At least it didn't say 'Crymore'. Am I right?" whilst raising an eyebrow. The team shook their heads as Shake says "No. Don't be silly. It can't be Crymore- Crymore died! Whatever it was, it's gone for now and I don't doubt we will see it again."

"I'll get a few of my best guys to investigate the forest to see if there's anything suspicious in there" announced Rix, tipping his beanie. "We have two days before the Fruit and Veg festival. I suggest we stay on our guard, stay in a group and keep working - we'll do more studying after Woodroes' birthday." The team agreed as they carried on their jobs in bigger groups whilst being on full alert, not wanting to delay the famous Fruit and Veg festival – Woodroes' birthday.

~ ~ ~

It's the day of the Fruit and Veg festival and everyone is excited and all dressed up. Everyone is having a grand time! The events of the other day somewhat washed over them due to the amazing atmosphere Amber was giving out. Shake and Nikita are nattering and bickering like always by the fruit punch, Rix and Vanessa Lamb are letting Gigglesworth Jr try new fruits and veg whilst talking to their new neighbours about Hamsters.

Vanessa Lamb has recently bought Gigglesworth Jr a Hamster. Gigglesworth Jr has been having-awful nightmares that includes swirling purple and magenta colours and paper, so when he arises at night he can have fun with his new nocturnal buddy to sweeten his dreams. Rix instantaneously named it "Little Furry Dude", Rix seems to love it more than Vanessa Lamb and Gigglesworth Jr combined!

The Colossi are having fun too! The children (And some adults!) are keeping Funple busy with all his exciting traits, Farad is running around racing people, Amber and Bubbles are bickering like Shake and Nikita and Daniel Comrade is texting in the corner, enjoying a fruit cocktail. It is now into the night time celebrations and the party starts kicking hard. Cecilia Ramaysa is wandering around the party recording it and editing it as she goes along, adding some funny effects to the footage with her well-armed bodyguards; she stops recording however when Daniel walks up to her looking rather disheartened.

"What's wrong my love? Is everything okay?" asked a rather concerned Cecilia.

"I'm afraid I'm having a relationship issue Cecilia and I was wondering if I can have some advice? Who better to ask than a super computer, ya'know? Ahaha..." Daniel said nervously, shaking his cocktail.

"Yeah sure hun, more than happy to help! Hope it's nothing too serious, what is it?" replied Cecilia.

"I have a boyfriend who was a very bad man- he's changed now though he realized the error of his ways. He has this 'friend' who treats him very badly - abusive in fact. I've tried to intervene but this 'friend' threatens me every time with dark horrific promises. What should I do?" said Daniel as he necks the remains of his cocktail.

Cecilia, rather confused, replies "Abuse is never acceptable. I would take your partner to one side and talk it through with him. He doesn't need someone like that supposed "friend" of his. He's got everything he needs already, a handsome helicopter military man who's smile could break a thousand hearts!" Dan tears up a little as he walks away, after thanking Cecilia Ramaysa.

Barry then approaches Cecilia Ramaysa, Cecilia says in a very cheery tone "Barry love! How're you doing my good friend?" Barry jiggles and giggles with happiness, "Why don't you guys have a break and enjoy the party?" says Cecilia to her bodyguards "I should be safe when in the company of THE brave, Blissful Barry." she added. Her guards nod and trundle towards the veggie feast hand in hand. Cecilia and Barry walk side by side "So, what's going on Barry? Everything okay?" asks Cecilia, Barry nods and smiles, whilst looking over at Vanessa Lamb, Rix, Gigglesworth Jr and Little Larry. "You want a proper family, don't you love?" Barry somewhat blushes through his fleshy exterior and nods, "Well, whoever ends up with you Barry will be one lucky Colossi! You're handsome, brave and very, very cute!" Cecilia says in an enthusiastic jolly tone. Barry dances with happiness, giggles then stands up on his hind legs and gives Cecilia a huge hug, making sure that none of his golden spikes touch Cecilia. Cecilia notices Liquid Negativity slowly seeping from Barry due to his excitement. "Ohh, think its Little Larry's feeding time!" Barry smiles, nods in approval and walks away with a bounce in his step towards his lovable son, Little Larry, who is super excited to see him and starts filling the vicinity with positive gas whilst being fed.

Cecilia Ramaysa lets out a graceful sigh before hearing movement in the bushes behind her. She turns around and does a scan and detects the same name that the Saviours mentioned – "CRYBORG". Before Cecilia could shout or scream, an electric net flies towards her and wraps her up! Lisa and Amy are the first to notice and shout "What's happening to Cecilia!?" The Saviours and Colossi all run to her aid and see the steel culprit, whilst Daniel Comrade gets all the civilians out of the vicinity.

Approaching the distressed Cecilia Ramaysa was none other than the nearly unrecognisable Dr. Crymore! Equipped with a sharp robotic right-hand steel claw, a high-tech liquid cannon, powerful rocket boots and a chamber full of Fury Fluid connected to his back - he appeared to be 75% robot. As Crymore stood in front of Cecilia, Shake clenches his fist and shouts "Crymore!"

He ran towards him with great speed, blinded by rage at the vivid memory of the murder of his best friend Larry Little. The Saviours shouted "Shake, no!" as he screamed.
"You killed my best friend!" the second he got close to Crymore, Crymore quickly swiped his robotic claw across Shakes belly, sending him flying to the ground barely alive! The team gasped as Nikita Blue faints.

Vanessa Lamb screams "Crymore, you monster! How could you!? You're supposed to be dead!" Crymore hovers and shouts in a misshapen robotic tone. "Idiots! I am no longer Dr. Crymore, I am the ultimate weapon - CRYBORG! I have come for Cecil-" before Cryborg could finish, Barry's golden spiked filled tail smashes into Cryborg's vulnerable chest! Cryborg gets sent flying into a tree in the forest. Barry stomped with anger on the floor, dropping Liquid Negativity around the area right next to Shake!

The other Colossi approached Cryborg looking very intimidating in their own unique way whilst Larry and Cecilia's bodyguards try to get Cecilia freed. Rix and Vanessa Lamb took care of Nikita and Gigglesworth Jr. Shivy ran over and carried Shake to safety, trying to avoid the Liquid Negativity around the area. Cryborg gets up, smirks, wipes the blood off his chest where a golden spike had pierced him and thus, the battle was on.

One by one, the Colossi's were defeated; Amber couldn't get passed Cryborg's fire resistance and received a horrible scar to the chest by his sharp claw, Bubbles couldn't hit Cryborg due to taking a blast of Fury Fluid to the face and down his long neck, Lisa and Amy tried to charge into Cryborg together but with his impeccable speed, he successfully dodged them as they collided into a tree. Farad joined Amy and Lisa by charging but much like Amy and Lisa, his attack was dodged as he ran into the transporting twins and gave them both a bad electric shock. Funple, being the big purple giant, swung his incredible great giant, childless fist down to crush Cryborg but with him being so slow, Cryborg dodged and knocked Funple down with multiple blasts of Fury Fluid to the legs, chest and face. Funple collapsed onto the forest, flattening many trees.

Woodroe turned to Barry and said, "Let's take him down together ol' chum!" As they stampeded towards Cryborg, he punched Woodroe in the chest with his claw. Barry swung his tail towards Cryborg but Cryborg used his rocket boots to fly out of the way, allowing Barry's tail to smash against Woodroe!

Cryborg flew over the unconscious Colossi and towards Cecilia. Little Larry, in complete fear, ran towards Barry who was trying to help Woodroe up. Cecilia's guards were left shaking in fear- if the Colossi couldn't stop him there's no chance they could! But, being the brave men they were, they held out their electro halberds and pointed them at Cryborg, knowing full well they stood no chance. Cryborg aimed his cannon at the guards, after one blast they managed to get their weapons blown from their hands and were sent flying backwards, somehow like a miracle, not getting a single drop of Fury Fluid on their skin. This left Cecilia Ramaysa defenceless. Cryborg picked up the net and hovered in the air, looked at the destruction he had caused and then flew away with the Colossi in hand, to which Daniel ran to the field shouting "No wait, stop!" but it was too late.

The Fruit and Veg fair was a complete disaster; the Saviours were hospitalised and the Colossi were recovering in "*Colossinfirmary*". Vanessa Lamb and Rix are consoling Daniel Comrade and Nikita is beside Shake who is in critical condition and lucky to be alive.

The next day…

Daniel walks in holding a card and some flowers and places them next to Shakes bed. Nikita gets up as the two leave the room to discuss what's happening.
"How's the big guy doing?" asked Daniel who is noticeably concerned and shaking.
"The reports say that the cuts were extremely deep, if it weren't for Shivy getting him help in time he wouldn't have survived. The doctors said he should make a full recovery. Thanks to Shake's natural remedies that he had shared with the doctors, it'll be no time at all for him to get back on his feet. Did you not read the record?" replied Nikita.
Daniel sighed with relief, "Sorry, I hadn't had time." He then gave Nikita a much needed, tight hug. Shivy was walking down the hallway, Nikita pushed Daniel off her and jumped on her fiancée's saviour, Shivy, wrapping her arms around her like a boa constrictor and thanking her for looking out for Shake and risking her life for him. Shivy said in an emotional tone, "I'm so happy he is okay!" whilst clapping her hands excitedly. "How are you doing Nikita? I saw you had fainted and you banged your head?" she added.

"I'm fine really, don't worry – I have other things to worry about at the moment" replied Nikita.

Meanwhile in Shakes room, Shake awakens, sits on his bed and reads the cards that his friends have left him.

"Get well soon dude, I know a guy who can get you some fantastic pain reliefs, just say the word and its yours! All the best man, love Rix, Vanessa and Gigglesworth Jr. xxxx"

"Well, I guess you owe me one huh? May put this debt into use when I'm next on hot-beverage duty – so many orders to remember! I hacked into the records (I know they're accessible to us but, I just do it for the thrill really...) and found out you're going to pull through! So happy! Get well soon Shakey! Lots of love from Shivy xxx"

"Get well soon, bud. - Dan the Man."

He gets up with a smile after reading the cards and heads to the bathroom where he starts to remove his ward gown (even by pulling off the ward-gown –he manages to create a fashion statement) to find something behind his ear, a black wet substance that wiped off like custard - Shakes eyes widened in shock, "Its Liquid Negativity!" he exclaims!

He screams and collapses on the floor in terror! Nikita, Shivy and Daniel run into the room to see Shake on the floor looking up at the mirror.

Daniel picks up the distraught Shake and places him on the bed. Nikita asks "What's going on Shake!? Is everything okay!?" Shake catches his breath, looks at his scar on his stomach and then bursts out laughing!

Shivy rather concerned says "I think we should leave him alone for a while, he needs some time to himself..." As Shivy, Daniel and Nikita are slowly walking towards the door to get a nurse, Shake shouts "Eureka!" They turn around to see Shake slamming himself on the bed laughing more, turning over Daniel's cheap card and scribbling on its back: *"I know a way to prevent the effects of Liquid Negativity!"* in awful handwriting, all the while gasping for air and tears streaming down his face.

Daniel, Shivy and Nikita gasp! "How!?" demanded Shivy and Nikita.

Shake calms himself down, still chuckling away and sniffling. "Near death experiences! Crymore nearly died back at his lab and he was drenched in the stuff, I've certainly nearly died and yet – I too, am immune!"

Nikita, confused, asks "But Shake... how do you know you're immune?"

He giggles and says, "Ohh, because of this!" and folds back his ear revealing some semi-dry liquid negativity. Nikita and Shivy gasp, followed by a burst of tears by Nikita. "Please tell me you are immune, I can't go through losing you! Certainly, after nearly losing you yesterday!" Shake cheerfully gets out of bed, swabs off the liquid negativity with a tissue and burns it with his lighter, he then walks towards Nikita and gives her a big hug saying, "I feel fantastic Nikita. If I was affected I wouldn't be here right now." Nikita grabs hold tighter and she says gently to him, "I'm so happy you're alive. Just don't do anything that stupid ever again, okay!?"

If there was one thing Shake was terrified of, it was an angry Nikita. Somehow her tone and words pass right through him and hit him where it hurts. He surely learns his lessons when it's Nikita teaching them. However, this doesn't stop

Shake from being stubborn and trying to win an already lost battle.

Daniel Comrade states in a low tone "I'm sorry to break this up guys but we have some business we need to discuss, like the disappearance of Cecilia Ramaysa?"

Shake jolts up and says "Cecilia's gone!?" his scar starts hurting as he sits up on the bed in pain.

"You need to rest my darling. Once you're rested up we can get a plan to get her back!" says Nikita, concerned.

Shake, being a smart young man, nods in agreement and says "Yes, I am exhausted. Please go tell the others about the immunity to Liquid Negativity, they need to know. I need to rest up a bit."

After giving Shake a kiss on the cheek, Nikita and her best friend Shivy go and tell the others about the immunity to Liquid Negativity and Shake's recovery. Daniel went to get ready for the meeting and to tell the Colossi of Shakes condition and discovery. Oh, how the Colossi cheered! It certainly helped them recover.

The Colossi, being built with great endurance, recovered rather quickly. They had a team dressed from head to toe in hazmat suits, washing and scrubbing away the Fury Fluid. Not one drop can remain on them as it can start a whole massacre. Barry felt incredibly guilty for striking Woodroe during the commotion, so he and Little Larry walked out and fetched him some flowers, bark and a card telling him to get well soon. Woodroe certainly appreciated the gesture.

Three days later, Shake left the hospital completely recovered and the Colossi are out doing their own jobs. Shake holds a meeting with The Saviours and Colossi: "Before we start, I would just like to wish Woodroe a happy birthday! I am so sorry that your party didn't go as planned and terrible events occurred. Once this mission is over, we will have a Fruit and Veg fair weekend! None-stop, how does that sound?" Oh, how the Saviours cheered! Woodroe bowed, "Thanks Shake. That means a lot. I am so happy you're all better," he said as he was curling his moustache.

"I'm better in many ways! I've been some-what upgraded with the gift of being immune to Liquid Negativity! Did everyone hear about that?" enquired Shake. Everyone agreed and showed great delight.

"Let's get down to business. Cecilia Ramaysa has been kidnapped by none other than Crymo-no, Cryborg. Does anyone know where he has flown too?" asks Shake.

"He flew north-west!" said Shivy.

"Isn't that where Dr. Gigglesworth's lab? is?" enquired Nikita.

"His brother's old lab could be his stronghold... I wouldn't put it past him if he's set up there. All of Gigglesworth's chambers and laboratory equipment remains there...." said Rix, raising an eyebrow.

"I believe I saw him fly south!" interrupted Daniel Comrade with no hesitation at all, "Towards the old mines..." he added.

Shake said "Well, we have two possible directions - North-West and South! Right, Daniel, Amy and Amber, I want you three to scout the land, if you see anything, head back to headquarters and report to Vanessa Lamb, who will be in constant communication with us via text messages, phone calls may give us a way.

Shivy and Nikita, I want you two to hold fort here, make sure everything's under control with the civilians and Colossi. Rix, you go South an investigate the old mines with Farad and Bubbles, again, report anything unusual. As for me, I'm taking Barry and Larry with me to Dr. Gigglesworth's lab! Any objections?"

Nikita shows some concern as Shake has only just recovered, also Barry looked incredibly nervous about revisiting the start of his cuddly rampage. "You just left the hospital three days ago, do you think it's wise to be going to a potential stronghold in your condition?" asks Nikita.

"Absolutely yes, I feel as fit as a fiddle. I'm also with Barry, who's by far our strongest fighter so I will be fine and protected. Ain't that right, buddy?" Shake replies. Barry nods as Larry climbs atop of Barry and giggles. "You okay going back to the lab, Barry? I mean, it's where you were-" before Shake could finish, Barry does a big nod and Little Larry nearly falls off his head! They share a giggle and continue planning.

As Shake, Barry and Larry are walking up the hillside through the forest beneath the tree's, Barry spots a family of ducks and ducklings waddling passed and two adult sheep with two lambs staring at them from the cliff-side up ahead. He lets out a cheery sigh as Little Larry giggles and pats him on the head. Shake taps him on his front leg and says, "I've noticed you've been eyeing up Vanessa Lamb, Rix and Giggleworth Jr. You want a family, don't you? A wife and a mother to Little Larry, right?" Barry giggles, blushes and nods, "One day my friend you will have your wish, you just have to be patient!" Shake says as he giggles. "Ohh look! We're almost there!" he added as he points towards the huge laboratory up ahead, his phone vibrates as Shake gets a text message from Nikita.

"If we have Porkberry Pie for tea, would you like Apple-Carrot crumble for afters? We have no custard, but I was able to get some Porkberry sauce from

the markets which I think goes better with Apple-Carrot crumble than custard.
Love you, be safe xxx"

Shake responded:
"Sounds great however custard always triumphs over any saucy toppings to any
dessert."

Shake wanted to make a point with the lack of kisses at the end of the text, showing Nikita that truly, she was wrong and that no other desert topping is better than custard.

They get to the laboratory which is covered in graffiti, police tape and plant life - this building has obviously been abandoned for quite a fair while. Shake sees that the door to the lab is slightly ajar, followed by small drips of fury fluid on the floor. "Cyborg is obviously here!" Shakes says through gritted teeth to Barry and Larry. Shake slightly opens the door a bit more and squeezes through, he opens it a bit more so Barry can walk in. Barry takes one step inside, turns left and sees the chamber where he was created, covered in his dried blood and dried Liquid Negativity. Flashbacks come straight to Barry as he remembers his horrendous loved-filled massacre and the death of his creator, Dr. Gigglesworth.

He shrieks and stamps around, drawing a lot of attention to themselves! Larry in a flash leaps onto his back and suckles on Barry's negativity spewing spikes, releasing the positive gas calming Barry down. They hear a door open in the distance followed by a rigid voice, "Who's there!? Show yourself!"
Shake whispers to Larry "Giggle, Little Larry!", Larry starts giggling along with Shake as they run out. The rigid voice then mutters "Blasted kids again! Don't come back! I'm the fabled Horrendo the Hobo! OoooooOOOOhhhh!" and

the door slams shut.

Horrendo the Hobo was a rumour spread around by kids and teenagers whose apparently living at the discontinued lab of Dr. Gigglesworth. Whoever's living here is either a harmless hobo not wanting to be disturbed or someone far worse.

Shake is shocked to know that the Laboratory is still in somewhat operation, the fact that there was Fury fluid at the scene makes it that much more suspicious and pin-points that Cryborg is in there somewhere. Shake, whilst outside the laboratory sends a text message to Nikita Blue saying:

"Dr. Gigglesworths lab is still in use! there was Fury Fluid right outside the lab which leads me to believe that Cryborg is in there."

~ ~ ~

Whilst Shake is sending the text and Barry is outside calming down, inside the lab, Cecilia Ramaysa is wired up and unable to move. A male figure in a lab coat with extremely long and wild black matted hair is standing in front of her giggling to himself. Cecilia shudders. On her chest there's a screen, showing that a text is being sent from right outside the lab - in a flash, this unknown male professor forces Cecilia to open the message and display it! After being given horrendous painful shocks to her back, Cecilia couldn't help but reveal the message. "Ha! Idiot! He thinks he can rescue Cecilia! What a joke! Cryborg, get here now, you beautiful tinman ahaha!"
Cryborg emerges from the shadows and says in his normal, deep, musky voice, "Yes, what is it?"

"I need you to put Cecilia Ramaysa in the travel cage - we need to get out of here as that blasted Shake is onto us!" says the professor.

"Yes." replies Cryborg.

"What was that, Cryborg!? You're a robot remember!?"

Cryborg lets out a sigh.

"Affirmative."

As Shake, Barry and Larry are heading down the hill to get back to the town, they hear weird rustling noises, mechanical movements and laughter followed by the smell of AppleCarrot Crumble with Custard coming from behind the laboratory. Shake, Barry and Larry investigate quietly, sneaking in the direction in which they had seen them!

Cecilia Ramaysa, all wired up in an electric cage, wheeling next to Cryborg and a professor with long black shoulder-length hair, devouring AppleCarrot Crumble and Custard. Barry, seeing Cecilia Ramaysa in a cage, similar to what he was trapped in, awoke some bottled up rage inside of him. Barry charged in after them, slamming his fleshy spike covered tail into Cryborg, once again flinging him into a tree!

"Argh! Will you stop that, please!?" Cryborg shouts in a stuttering tone.

The Professor drops his crumble and says "Ahh, boulderdashery! Its Shake! I thought you were investigating my lab with your band of tools!"

Shake jumps out, "I was going to get back up!" announces Shake.

Although being a professor with a PHD in "Complicated Mathematics" and a Masters in "Evil Naughty Science", he was not one for common sense, giving into demanding cravings for AppleCarrot Crumble before putting any strategic thought into his own safety – but who wouldn't?

Luckily for Shake, he's quite flat when it comes to text messaging, not really giving much details. The lack of "Tell the others" and "We're going in!" made the professor hazard a guess if he already has back-up or not. Sadly, this was not the case.

"Who are you!? And what are you doing with Cecilia Ramaysa and Cryborg!?" he questioned demandingly.
"Smart young man! I am Professor Determinill! I saved Cryborg here from his impending doom when you attempted to kill him! Cryborg, get up you dreamy worthless band of bolts!" Determinill shouts as he gets out an electric whip.

Cryborg gets up and hesitantly aims his cannon at Shake, "Haha! I'm immune to your liquids and fluids, I know the cure!" shouts Shake in a proud manner. Cryborg shudders as he remembers striking Shake across the belly, not finishing him off. Determinill, very angrily, glares at Cryborg and says "Idiot! you nearly killed him!?" Cryborg cringes and says with a slight stutter "S-Sorry, even you sa-aaid he should of bled to de-eaath. You were contro-olling me-e for that s-siege too. I can hardly remember wha-at happened tha-at night."
"Don't you even THINK about blaming me, you useless but gorgeous weapon!" responded Determinill, clutching his whip with fury. Before he could strike Cryborg with the whip, a big clash was heard after their blazing argument as Barry swung his tail and destroyed the cage, saving Cecilia Ramaysa.

Shake turns back around and notices Professor Determinill hopping onto Cryborg's back. Cryborg hovers in the air as Professor Determinill exclaims in excitement "Ha! I no longer need Cecilia Ramaysa, she was merely going to be a hostage if you tried anything! I have this!" he reveals a silver flash drive, with an obscure logo on it. Cryborg launches in the air and flies away, Professor Determinill's manic laughter fading away.

Cecilia thanks Barry and Shake greatly as she cuddles Little Larry. She informs them that Professor Determinill has copied some files from her, the files being: "How to make a Colossi", "Footage of the Fruit and Veg Fair" and "Top notch recipe for AppleCarrot Crumble and Custard". Shake shakes his head and announces: "We must inform the others." They head up to Dr. Gigglesworth's old lab and contacted Daniel Comrade to pick them up. Shortly after, Amy and Lisa arrive with the Saviours followed by Daniel in his helicopter with an attached platform for Cecilia Ramaysa.

Cecilia climbs upon the platform and Daniel gets into his helicopter like a man who has the weight of everyone's worries on his back, dragging down a cigarette. Barry and Larry climb into Lisa whilst the Saviours fly in Amy right behind Daniel in his chopper. Shake begins explaining what had happened at the scene with this new psychotic criminal mastermind.

As they fly from the lab to the town, the team have another intense meeting, whilst celebrating that they were able to successfully save Cecilia. "I still can't believe Crymore is still alive," announces Vanessa Lamb. "He looked pretty dead when we left him covered in that rubble and Liquid Negativity..." she added.
"Makes you wonder how he escaped I mean, that Determinill fellow looked very lanky..." Said Shake,
"What do you mean, darling?" asked Nikita.

"Think about it, he was missing many limbs and near enough bleeding to death covered in rubble - someone had to have known his exact location to have saved him in time and have the strength to remove the debris..." he added.

"What are you talking about? What would possess someone to risk their lives to save a man like that?" questioned Daniel over the phone, dragging on his sixth cigarette.

"Maybe it was an act of love..." intervenes Cecilia, over the phone.

The atmosphere goes silent, but as they get closer to home - the team suddenly hears Amber's roar yet again, coming from the town centre.

The Saviours land the helicopter in a designated zone in the town centre near Funple, who looks very distracted, looking up at the beautiful summer night sky shining upon his spotlights. As they looked beyond Funple, to their horror... they noticed the town is in pure panic!

Funple is shining lights across the sky, claiming he saw some kind of "lilac bat creature" launching Fury Fluid out of its tail at the civilians from the sky! Luckily no one has been hit and now, lucky for the civilians, Barry and the other Colossi can jump in front of the great balls of Fury Fluid, taking the hits to avoid it getting in contact with the people. The placements of where the Fury Fluid had hit intrigued Nikita- they were very peculiar. On the roofs and in the forested areas, almost like maybe, warning blasts?

Woodroe, Amy and Lisa gathered up as many civilians as they could and escorted them into the none hazardous woods where they'll be safe. Barry and Larry follow as they spread positive gas to calm everyone down. The flying lilac beast screeches as it gets caught in Funple's lights! The creatures skin glitters in such dark beauty and its eyes glow a beautiful yellow like that of a moon and its wing-span of incredible length! But before they could get a good look at the creature, they noticed a recognisable, unsymmetrical silhouette on the back of the creature as it then swiftly flew away after launching one more blast of Fury Fluid just five meters in front of the Saviours.

Bubbles, in an instant, gets to work washing the town clean of the Fury Fluid whilst Woodroe manipulates the trees to make temporary houses for the Civilians. The team get together and discuss what they had saw whilst watching Cecilia's recorded footage. Shake, in complete concern says, "This must be the work of that Professor Determinill and Cryborg!"
"We need to find them, they've left the lab they must be working somewhere else!" announces Rix.
"This is getting really bad, I want it all to stop!" Shivy exclaims in complete panic, tears welling up in her eyes.
"This was clearly a test run, imagine when that thing is loose!" says Nikita.

Cecilia looks at Daniel Chopper Comrade and simply nods.

I have a confession to make..." Daniel says as he walks up to the group. "Crymore is my lover," he adds, stubbing out his seventh cigarette.

The Saviours recoil in shock and confusion. Rix, in complete rage goes to attack Daniel but Cecilia knocks him back with her tail. "Let him finish!" she shouts.

"Traitor!" he screams as he glares at his comrade.

Daniel Comrade brushes off Rix's attack and glare, "Before you guys stormed the government's stronghold, I was seeing Dr. Crymore. We met up for coffee and Dove Milk Sundaes every other day. We could talk for hours and hours - I had no idea he had captured Barry and was using his Liquid Negativity to create weaponry - I just thought he had a boring desk job..."

"Get to the point man!" demands Rix, getting up from the dirt to tightly hug Gigglesworth Jr and Vanessa Lamb, who just arrived at the scene.

"When you called me to pick you guys up Rix, I headed straight over in concern for your safety. When I had got there amongst the rubble, I saw Crymore, laying in a pool of Liquid Negativity and blood - my heart was broken! Once I dropped you guys off at your base, I quickly returned to the scene as fast as I could - I couldn't help myself! I wore some protective clothing that I had stored in my helicopter and dragged the limp body of Crymore from the debree and rubble to the back seat, in which Crymore muttered the word "Sorry..." as we lifted off. I took him to a good friend of mine - Professor Nigel Determinill, who had taught me science in school...."

Shake's cigarette drops out of his mouth in awe, while Shivy starts shuddering as the story thickens.

"Professor Determinill instantaneously got to work in saving Crymore's life. Once I told him about the effects of Liquid Negativity, which I overheard you guys talking about on our journey to your base, Determinill quickly realized that a near-death experience prevents Liquid Negativity's effects..."

Stomping on his dropped lit cig, shouts in pure anger "Wait! You knew how to prevent Liquid Negativity and you never told us!?"

Catching a breath, Daniel continues.

"After constructing a robotic figure to the now alive Crymore, Determinill says that he had placed a bomb within Crymore and stated that if we don't pay him back by doing 'a few favours', he will detonate the bomb which could take out the town. In complete fear we accepted; he said that once the favours are met we could be together and he will take out the bomb."

A tear streams down Shivy's face as Gigglesworth Jr starts to fall asleep in Rix's arms.

"...Determinill was fascinated by Liquid Negativity and experimented ways of 'improving' its malicious effects. He tried adding many things to the liquid like tea-leaves and custard, but then he discovered a way. The Kamikaze Khemical, freshly extracted from Kamikaziants."

The Saviours gasped as they all sat around Daniel and Cecilia like school children listening to a children story book.

"Throughout the years that had passed while Shake and Vanessa Lamb were constructing the Colossi, Determinill was treating Crymore like a weapon, getting him to steal and pillage without leaving a trace. He caused many riots and suicides over the years but this was mainly due to Determinill having the ability to hack into him; when Crymore refuses to do anything he got punished by Determinill's high voltage electric whip."

Barry started to shudder, unable to tear up due to being inside out, frustrated he shook on the spot, relating to being treated like a weapon.

"Crymore has told me he realizes what he had done in the past was wrong, the way he treated Barry, the way he wanted to introduce Liquid Negative Weaponry, how he wanted to take over the world. He was blinded by power and jealousy of his successful brother, Dr. Gigglesworth."

Gigglesworth Jr wakes up and lets out a little cheer and clap as he heard his name.

"Determinill wants to make the ultimate weapon to replace Crymore once he no longer needs him, I believe the creature we had just witnessed is that weapon which he wanted to create."

Daniel Comrade starts to finally tear up.

"Crymore has told me that he wants to turn over a new leaf. He knows what he has done cannot be undone but he will do everything in his power to make things right. He must find a way of getting passed Determinill's hack and the bomb. If you guys are willing to help save my boyfriend, I can tell you where they're now based. Crymore will help us out."

"When at the lab, I saw how cruelly Determinill acted towards Crymore, he really didn't want to commit any new horrors he just wanted to leave. Crymore looked at me and all I saw was pain, I didn't even need to scan. I believe him. I will do everything in my power to help him out and if you're the Saviours that I think you are, you will too." announces Cecilia Ramaysa.

Shake stands up and says "There is no other way around it, I accept. Who else is up for taking down another insane criminal?"

The team stand up and nod. Daniel Comrade cries with happiness, "Thank you guys."

The Saviours discussed the plans as Daniel tells them "I have had confirmation off Crymore, he says that they are still at Dr. Gigglesworth's laboratory. Determinill assumed that we would think that they would have moved location."
"Daniel, go to Dr. Gigglesworths lab on your own and distract Determinill, me and the others will find a way in and we'll catch him when he least expects it," orders Rix in a very enthusiastic, but still aggressive tone. All the Saviours, Barry, Larry, Cecilia, Funple, Farad and Woodroe headed to Gigglesworth's lab that very evening.
When they reached the lab they realized that this time the door is locked shut

with no lock to pick. Nikita, being the lands best gadgeteer, plants a bomb by the door; before the explosion Funple used his very unique ability to eat the sound of the explosion - keeping their whereabouts a secret. As they opened the now heavily damaged door, the Saviours ran in and went down the stairs in search of the basement whilst Barry, Larry and Cecilia stayed outside. Funple headed back home to amuse the civillians and Woodroe started growing trees around the lab ready to bury it in greenery. The Saviours walked passed the chambers with such determination and found the basement.

~ ~ ~

Meanwhile, outside, Cecilia is comforting Barry as he doesn't feel comfortable being in the lab where he was born. "You can't keep running from your past Barry, what's done is done, it can't be undone. The Saviours need you in there..." says Cecilia Ramaysa.
"You're the strongest, smartest and most heroic Colossi I know Barry, get in there and help your friends who saved you!" exclaims Woodroe in his typical old English accent. Larry jumps on the back of Barry and pats him on the back as Barry nods in approval. He faces the lab and walks in, shaken but brave.

Cecilia follows him in as he starts getting flash backs of what he was like all those years ago. He sees his dried up Liquid Negativity all over the walls, he can see the imprints on the ground from when he stomped, he sees Dr. Gigglesworth's old dusty lab coats and then he goes into the next room where he sees *it*.

Determinill's beautiful lilac weapon, laying in the Chamber where Barry was created, chained up and pinned down by claws receiving electrical shocks every few seconds to anger and torture the poor beast. The glass is soundproof, but you can see her shrieking in pain from behind the chamber. Cecilia and Larry followed him in and saw this horrendous sight. As Barry's body tenses up in anger, Barry stampedes in a blind rage and bursts through the front of the chamber completely shattering the front. He swings his tail and with such force, sending the lilac weapon out of the front of the chamber and breaking the chains.

The Lilac Weapon lays on the ground in front of the chamber like a wounded animal, staring at her hero standing in the very chamber that Barry was born in.

Barry looks up and sees the claw, the very same claw which is drenched in Barry's dried-up blood. The claw which had turned him into the creature he is now. The claw attempted to grab him, but ended up going inside of him and like that moment all those years ago; blood, screams, Liquid Negativity and steam fills the chamber. Larry and Cecilia cry out as they witnessed the end of Boggy Barry, the redeemed masterpiece.

The Lilac weapon approaches the chamber and bows with tears in her neon yellow eyes. The three of them leave the lab mourning for their fallen hero.

As they leave, Cecilia Ramaysa breaks down and asks the lilac weapon to help the Saviours – it's something Barry would have done. The weapon bows down to Cecilia Ramaysa and gives off a soft purr, "Carrie? What a cute name!" she says in an enlightened tone with a hint of sorrow.

Little Larry is weeping over the loss of his father and his tummy rumbles, Carrie spurts out a little bit of Fury Fluid and Little Larry has a little feast.

Carrie has a very similar shape and structure to Barry, she has a beautiful glittering Lilac coat with beautiful magenta hair, she has a fringe covering one of her yellow neon eyes. Her chest is fury like a shaggy husky and she rocks two enormous bat wings. Much like Barry, she doesn't speak a specific language, just a series of purrs like a cat.

On her back, her structure has been melded into the shape of a seat with what looks to be a lilac artery, extending out the middle of her tail to the back. Her tail has a cannon on the end in the shape of a siphon, to which she can launch huge balls of Fury Fluid. She also has an artery coming out of her neck, to plug into Cryborg when low on ammunition (Fury Fluid). Her feet are like cat paws covered in magenta hair; she's extremely dexterous and nimble, she has fangs and a serpent tongue, purely for intimidation purposes.

~ ~ ~

Back in the basement, The Saviours over-hear the discussions between Determinill, Cryborg and Daniel Comrade. "I see how well you handled the creature. It's like you were born the ride it!" says Determinill.
"You got your weapon Determinill." says Daniel with frustration in his tone, "Now remove the bomb from Crymore so we can live together in peace and not be part of your evil plan.".
Determinill bursts out in laughter, "I'm sorry but Cryborg belongs to me now, consider yourself lucky that I'm allowing you to walk out of here alive!"
"Determinill. The weapon you have created can launch out giant balls of Fury Fluid at a rapid rate, you don't need me to be attached to the thing - I offer very little contribution." pleads Cryborg with distress in his tone.

Whilst the discussion was going on, Shivy was typing away on her tablet. She had successfully hacked into Cryborg's software and there was nothing in him which links to an explosive device - Determinill must be lying about the bomb. Shivy whispered the information to Shake, so Shake was then able to communicate this to Daniel via text message.

Daniel looked at his phone and grinned. Determinill got out his electric whip and shouted, "You're mine I tell you!" Before he could strike Cryborg, Daniel ran up to him and drop kicked Determinill square in the face! Determinill got up with one hand over his bruised face and got out his clipboard; it was full of buttons, notes and a silver flash drive plugged in. "I'll press the button! It will blow us all up if you're not careful!" shouts Determinill. At this point the Saviours burst in! "Not so fast Professor Determinill! We know your plans! Shivy hacked into Cryborg's system and found no link to any explosive devices, you're bluffing! " shouts Shake, "Where is that beast you created!?"

Determinill starts laughing more and says "Ohh, hello Saviours! It's a shame I don't have time to talk to you all because my weapon is on her way!" He pressed a Lilac button and started giggling with glee. Almost instantly they could hear flying coming from a behind the metal balcony door. Determinill presses a button on the wall and a metal door opens from the basement, revealing a window in the cliff side. There the Saviours witnessed the beautiful glittering lilac beast with glowing yellow eyes. Determinill demands, "Now Cryborg, mount the weapon!" he presses yet another button and Cryborg's eyes glow red. Cryborg instantly submits "Yes, at once master."
Daniel in complete shock shouts "Crymore, no!" before Daniel could dart towards Cryborg, Rix grabs hold of Daniel and says, "There's nothing you can

do! Cryborg will kill you if you get near him!"

Cryborg approached Carrie, the lilac winged weapon which has perched onto the window frame like a four-legged parakeet. Carrie looks at Cryborg with intensity, then pulls a very silly face when he got quite close. "Huh?" says both Cryborg and Determinill in confusion.

The weapon leaned its back and tail up revealing Little Larry mounting her back! Little Larry has his tail connected to Carries tail-artery, he then starts to drink the Fury Fluid from Carries neck-tube, and out of her tail streams out this glittery salmon-pink/violet plasmatic substance.

The plasma circulated the room, giving everyone, including Determinill, who has contact with the plasma a burst of motivation and positive feelings. This plasma however, had awoke Cryborg's mind freeing him from Determinill's hacking. Cryborg came back into reality, staring Carrie in the eyes. He bows to her and Larry as he turns very rapidly to Determinill aiming his cannon at him. "There's no bomb!?" cried Cryborg as his cannon arm shakes in anger.

The Saviours run behind Cryborg as they slowly got closer to Determinill who is quaking in his boots. Determinill starts nervously giggling and shaking saying "Cryborg... hehe... c'mon now, you're my hunky masterpiece! We were going to take over the world together! Besides hehe.... you know Fury Fluid won't affect me! I nearly died years ago so I can't be affected! So let's put the cannon down, okay big guy?"
"Yeah, you're right..." says Cryborg in an understanding manner. "But this can kill you!" he added, as he swiftly raises his razor-sharp claw arm.
Daniel grabs hold of Cryborgs arm and says "No! Don't do it! No more killing,

remember!?"

As Cryborg and everyone were distracted, Determinill did a very flashy and pretty cool back flip to the other end of the room- "You're all idiots! Do you really think I'd only make one weapon!?" he presses another button on his button-filled clip-board and the room started to shake. "Always have a back-up plan! Ahaha!" screeches Determinill.

The Saviours and Cryborg start to back up towards the window where Carrie and Larry are perched, while Determinill has yet another laughing fit. Out of the floor raised five huge chambers."Behold my Behemoths! Though they're not at 100% completion, these five are going to help me take over the world! You can keep that treacherous bat!" The Saviours gasped as the doors started opening. The room filled with steam and manic laughter as the creatures left the chambers.

"Woaaahh nelly! What do we 'ave 'ere den, Verminious!?" screeches one annoying voice which can only be described as a pre-pubescent 75 year-old, "I have no idea Minor Annoyity! They certainly look fun to play with!" says a dry, dirty, ratty, nasal voice with a hint of the dumb.

"Will you two be quiet, you're messing up our terrifying introduction!" says a dark toned voice that sounds like someone doing a comedic impression of Count Dracula.

"This one is cute, the yellow haired girl. She can hack, impressive." says a very seriously, "cool guy" like voice.

"Ahh quit your yapping! You're giving me a headache!" shouts a womanly voice who sounds like she's had one too many drinks, three kids who won't behave and has a never ending cold in the middle of a breakdown.

"Oh, can it yourself Fluencia, you're ruining the fun, you obnoxious water-bottle!" says the annoying voice.

The voices keep on laughing and giggling at each other like a group of crazy hyenas. Determinill is beside himself laughing along with them. The steam slowly starts to deteriorate as these "Behemoths" are revealed.

The vermin king, Verminious has a giant rat-like appearance with the same shape of a typical Colossi and is just downright ugly and grotesque. He eats absolutely anything and smells of moist aged cabbage and dried chicken feet that you can pick up from your local pet supplies shop. He can even stretch the limit of his stench to fill a large house. He also has an ability to control and summon many kinds of vermin such as rats, flies and pigeons to his side just by whistling. He's very slippery and flexible, allowing him the ability to squeeze through many kinds of pipes of all shapes and sizes. His two front teeth, though very apparent of being rat's teeth, are quite blunt and pretty useless.

We then have the queen of diseases - Fluencia! Fluenica has a Colossi and water-bottle like appearance with many tubes and arteries hanging off her, seeping with puss and many kinds of infections. Her attitude is very sluggish as she constantly feels under the weather, making her very easy to annoy and causing her to snap at anyone who so much as mildly aggravates her. Fluencia spreads diseases and infects the air around her; if she stays in the same place for long enough the place may have to be quarantined. Her tongue is actually a thermometer, that pokes out of her mouth when she speaks – Determinill clearly inputted this for the amusement of the other Behemoths.

Next up we have the terrifying Fearetical! Fearetical is the same shape of the typical Colossi on all fours, but bigger and made purely of lime-green slime! Fearetical is mainly the floating eye that swims around its body which is also full of bone-structures. Fearetical hates being physical, he just enjoys playing mind games and freaking people out and best of all - scaring people to the point of tears! He may not be the best at fighting, but when it comes to lowering your defence - there is no one better. His voice is often mocked as he does sound like a poor imitation of the Count, Dracula.

We then have the mischievous Rumoria Ganda! Rumoria Ganda is a ninja like Behemoth, who can hear you through six walls! He can put thoughts into your head whilst you sleep and make you believe things that you would not normally believe; he spreads rumours, leaks out secret information and he can do all this without being detected. He has a deep blue skin colour which changes its brightness to fit the colour of the sky and has very powerful suction cups on his fingers and toes, allowing him to attach to walls and hear valuable information with the help of his tail. Clearly, he is the brains out of the whole Behemoths.

And finally, Determinill's favourite - Minor Annoyity! Minor Annoyity is not a very impressive Behemoth; his only function is to annoy people and go great lengths to do so. He comes with many abilities such as being able to slowly drain battery life, manipulate traffic lights, move things to different locations without you knowing, steals singular socks, disconnect your Wi-Fi and completely slow down your downloading speeds. He has a very annoying laugh and he is completely unsymmetrical. He is simply a little prankster, he wears an annoying blue hoodie with the right sleeve rolled up and bright orange jogging pants with the left leg pulled up.

The Saviours faces just drop as they see these creatures slowly approach them.

"Look at them Fearetical! Look at their faces! They're so annoying and that's coming from me! Ahahahaha!" screams Minor Annoyit.

"Indeed, my good fellow! Look at that one with the blonde hair, I just want to COBBLE HER UP!" Fearetical says as he swiftly stretches towards Shivy, who then faints.

The Behemoths continue laughing aside from Rumoria Ganda who just rolls his eyes, "Determinill, why have you have released us this early? We're not complete yet.", Determinill climbs on top of Verminious, his fingers clutching against his sticky tacky fur. "Behemoths! You're all safe from the Lilac Weapon as her only real function is to fire Fury Fluid - something which you all aren't affected by! I want you all to take care of our guests, nothing can save them now!" shouts Determinill as he continues to laugh.

The Saviours are shaking in their boots completely stumped to what to do next. As the Behemoths get closer and more intimidating, the basement door flies off its hinges and knocks Minor Annoyity over - "Man that was annoying!" he exclaims.

Standing in the doorway is none other than Barry! He has been restored back to his original spongy design! Shivy awakens and the Saviours stand there even more speechless with big smiles on their faces. Behind Barry is Cecilia playing some epic heroic copyright free tunes!

"Determinill! Surrender yourself! What you see before you is the legendary Blissful Barry, the redeemed masterpiece!" she announces whilst Barry looks heroic and majestic. Little Larry in pure excitement drinks more Fury Fluid and more plasma fills the room. The Saviours, Carrie and Larry stand up to the Behemoths with their new feeling of motivation as Cryborg launches himself into the air, does a sweet somersault over the Behemoths and lands on Barry's back. Barry then starts to emit a very mysterious glow, noticeable but not alerting.

"I'm so happy to see you again, I am so sorry for the way I had treated you all those years ago - will you ever forgive me?"

Barry smiles and nods.

Determinill shouts "Behemoths! New target! Take out this Blissful Barry character!" The Behemoths gladly turn around.

"Fluencia have you seen this? This guy is made of sponges!" exclaims Fearetical as he lets out a dark foreboding giggle.

"Urgh, his overall appearance makes me want to puke, how ugly!" exclaims Fluencia, who is getting evils from the perching Carrie.

All but Verminious and Rumoria charge straight towards Barry and Cryborg. Barry defeats each and every one with great ease due to his fantastic strength and their incompleteness - they lay on the ground unable to fight! Minor Annoyity couldn't distract Barry because of Barry's impeccable patience for children, Fluencia was knocked back by Barry's intense donkey kick giving her the worst stomach cramps ever and Fearetical just melted in fear towards where Minor Annoyity laid!

Rumoria Ganda just walked to his chamber and leaned against it like nothing in this room is interesting him, avoiding any conflict with either parties knowing fine well he is incomplete and doesn't stand a chance.

Determinill laughs a bit more and shouts, "Whew! Quite the fighter aren't yah!? Defeating all my Behemoths! Verminious, operation turd fling!"

"Got it boss!" says Verminious with excitement in his voice. Verminious kicks his legs back like a Donkey, launching Determinill towards the Saviours!

Determinill drop kicks Nikita Blue right in the face and before anyone could grab hold of him, he goes through her pockets, pulls out a smoke bomb and uses it. The Saviours are in an intense coughing fit, Determinill grabs one more thing from Nikitas bag before jumping out onto the cliff-side window, avoiding Carrie and then begins climbing up the cliff towards the roof of the lab, laughing menacingly.

Carrie flies back a bit and flaps her wings rapidly to get rid of the smoke but Determinill was nowhere to be seen. Barry and Cryborg charge towards the Saviours knocking Verminious over and sending him smashing to the ground in the process. As Cryborg jumps down and gives Daniel a huge hug, Shake helps Nikita up and checks to see if she's okay. Vanessa Lamb and Rix check on Shivy who has just awoken from the fear and finally they all give Barry a huge hug!

Carrie looks Barry in the eyes and bows to Barry. Barry bows back and then Carrie gives Barry a cheeky kiss on his spongy cheek - Barry blushes and joyfully stamps around.

The Behemoths get up all in pain, "Where's Professor Determinill?" asks Minor Annoyity.
"Maybe he's gone to get us some medicine? I've got a splitting headache!" exclaims Fluenica, the other Behemoths laugh at the irony of Fluencia's comment. "I could hear him scampering up the side of the mountain. Pathetic, really." announces Rumoria Ganda who seems to be the only Behemoth with

sense.

"Guys, the fact that these people are staring us down is making me feel kind of... uncomfortable..." announces Fearetical who is building himself back up again.

Carrie climbs through the window and looks at the Behemoths, "Carrie! I thought it was you by the window - couldn't see as the sun was rising behind you, you looked like a giant bat silhouette! Ahahaha!" says Minor Annoyity. Carrie giggles and shakes her head.

"Where's Master Determinill at, Carrie?" asks Verminious.

"Don't you guys see? He's abandoned us." exclaims Rumouria Ganda rolling his eyes, "We are nothing but weapons to him." he adds. Carrie nods in agreement and the Behemoths gather together, "What do we do now then?" asks Verminious.

"You could come with us! No one gets left behind with us, we're one big happy family!" exclaims Cecilia in a loving tone, to which Barry turns around and nods in agreement.

"What a lovely offer tuts, give 'es a sec!" gargles Fearetical, the Behemoths gather together and have a group chat.

"You're a genius!" exclaims Verminious.

Rumoria walks over to Determinill's clipboard and picks it up, all the while the others approach the Saviours like children being forced to apologise to a neighbour, that they have been tormenting, by their strict parents. The Behemoths bow, the Saviours bowed back nervously thinking they're accepting a surrender, but then the Behemoths shout "SYKE!" Minor Annoyity turns out the lights as the Behemoths jump out of the window laughing among each other "Time to put our abilities to good use!" shouts Minor Annoyity as he rolls painfully down the cliff side.

The Saviours gasp "This is bad! They're going to destroy the world!" shouts Vanessa Lamb.

"Vermin will run riot in the streets, diseases will flood the land, fear will be around every corner and secrecy will be a thing of the past!" exclaims Rix in a mass panic. Carrie start to giggle.

"What's so funny!? This is serious!?" shouts Shake reaching for a cigarette, Carrie looks at Cecilia for a form of translation. She makes a cute purring noise to which Cecilia translates to, "They're not dangerous, they have their own agenda in mind" translates Cecilia, "The Behemoths were born way too early and their powers are very limited - if anything, their presence around the land would just be a minor annoyance. It's nothing we can't handle in the future." She adds.

"We have a much more pressing matter at hand at the moment, Determinill is still out there scaling the cliff side! Carrie, will you fly me up to the top?" asks Crymore.

 "I'm coming with you!" demands Daniel.

 "NO! This is my fight, I need to atone for my crimes." Crymore jumps onto Carries back, "I love you, Comrade."

Carrie takes flight and starts flying up to the top of the mountain, the roof of Gigglesworths lab.

"I love you too, William Crymore!" Daniel shouts back.

A small silence fills the room, before it was broken by a faint echoing from the sky "Its Giggleworth now aha! I'm no Crymore!" shouts back William.

The weather dramatically changes; there's heavy winds and rain pouring over the roof tops, the sun not yet reaching this height. Carrie makes it to the roof and at the very back of the roof is a silhouette of a man with long black dampened hair, clutching hold of a vibrant electric whip, sizzling in the rain. Carrie perches on the other side as the newly reformed Giggleworth gets off with burning anger in his eyes. Trees are rapidly growing around the sides of the lab due to Woodroes commands. Carrie flies back down to get the others.

"Nigel Determinill!" shouts William.
"William Crymore! It's about time you joined me on the roof, I was getting a little lonely and chilly! Weathers not the best, is it!?" shouted Nigel Determinill.

William blasts towards Nigel with his powerful jet boots "My name is Doctor William Gigglesworth!" he exclaims before tackling Determinill to the ground. Deterimill held onto William with a powerful grip, the pair started rolling around on the slippery rooftop.
"Why are you doing this Cryborg!?" demanded Deterimill as he struggles to get out of William's grasp.
"You poisoned my mind, you tortured me and you manipulated me! I wanted to change but you made me kill again!" exclaims William as thunder clashes onto the roof.

Deterimill launches William off him as he swings his whip, badly burning William's robotic claw! William aims his cannon at Deterimill and blasts Deterimill across the roof. Drenched in heavy Fury Fluid, Williams run towards Deterimill as he swings his whip one more time across Williams robotic face, burning it severely! Deterimill then gets up and jumps on top of William as they roll towards the edge of the roof. Deterimill is on top of William, covered in rain, tears, sweat and Fury Fluid. "There is no way I'm dying alone! We're going to die together, happy, laughing and smiling!" shouts Deterimill as he pulls out the laughing gas bomb he stole from Nikita and fills the area with laughing gas. The two start laughing to the point of tears. The Fury Fluid starts washing away as Deterimill grabs hold of William and says, "I've always loved you, Cryborg! You were my masterpiece!" but then suddenly, before Deterimill could roll both him and William off the edge, Daniel runs and knocks Deterimill with a mid-air drop kick off of the edge as he plummets to his grave, laughing.

Daniel wraps his arms around the crying, laughing William and they share a kiss. The Saviours and the Colossi are on the roof thanks to Carrie and Amy who had only just arrived. With the sinister mastermind, Professor Nigel Determinill gone, Daniel and William were able to be together finally.

~ ~ ~

A Year has passed since this fabled time, Daniel and William got married! Daniel is now known as Daniel Gigglesworth Chopper Comrade and William is now known as Doctor William Gigglesworth Comrade. Nikita has of course recovered from the quite brutal drop kick to the face, but she has good news on the way as she is expecting a baby with Shake! Dr. Gigglesworth's lab is now completely buried in greenery thanks to Woodroe and it is now the new location of the Fruit and Veg festival!

Professor Nigel Determinill's body was found entangled and pierced by branches with that still laughing face of his. He was buried in the local cemetery.

William's robotic limbs have been dismantled. Shake and Vanessa Lamb created prosthetic non-lethal limbs for William and an eye-patch instead of that robotic grinning face mask he was wearing.

Barry, Carrie and Little Larry are now a happy family and Gigglesworth Jr is getting older and smarter now. Vanessa Lamb and Rix can't wait to share these stories to him when he's old enough!

With some delightful experimentation, they had discovered that the plasma Larry makes when consuming Fury Fluid is motivational boosting, they had named it "Motivational Monoxide." Sadly however, the effects of Motivational Monoxide cannot dispel the effects of Liquid Negativity, it in fact encourages their suicidal tendencies.
Wonder what other substances Larry could convert?

With Blissful Barry now being "outside-in", Liquid Negativity and Fury Fluid is now a thing of the past, Shake is now able to create more Colossi that can benefit society and share them with the world with peace of mind - that is when Minor Annoyity stops moving his pens and notes!

Talking of the Behemoths, the Behemoths still hang around the city getting up to no good. Fearetical now lives in the dark forest next to Gigglesworth's lab, scaring people whenever he gets chance. Fluencia hangs around the mountain sides polluting the air spreading common colds and what not. Verminious has his own kingdom in the sewers under the town where he rules over vermin doing very little harm to the land above.

With new Colossi on the way, things are getting pretty exciting in the new city of Colossitopolis! Where the team have help evolve the small town of Sillitown into a famous city populated by good, honest people:

"WELCOME TO COLOSSITOPOLIS!
Home of the Colossi and winners of the AppleCarrot Crumble competition of 1670."

Dean Judd

Is a Sheffield based artist who practises with a long range of mixed media forms of art,
From paintings, character design, sewing and illustrations to pet product merchandise, fiction writing and caricaturist.
Dean is also a part of EYUP Curators Collective as a Workshop-Coordinator and Curator.

www.tattooedteabag.com

Facebook: Tattooedteabag Artwork
Instagram: tattooedteabag
Twitter: @tattooedteabag

www.ingramcontent.com/pod-product-compliance
Lightning Source LLC
Chambersburg PA
CBHW050413030726
47503CB00006B/2173